The Evanescence of Being

Barry Huggins

Published by Aquus Publishing, London
www.aquuspublishing.com

ISBN 978-0-9928893-1-9

First Edition: April 2014

For Sarah,
forever my soul mate,
my inspiration,
my guiding light.

The greatest illusion is the one
we perpetuate as our reality

Chapter One

Simon slouched over his desk and stared hypnotically at the dark film of pollution that coated the outside of the window. The clouds had been threatening all day and when they unleashed their storm it fell like black rain that carved streaks of charcoal rivers through the dirty glass. He forced himself out of his reverie and glanced at his watch for the fifth time in as many minutes. It was nineteen minutes past four. Just one more hour to go. He knew checking his watch repeatedly did not hasten the passage of time, but the activity calmed his mind and distracted him from the tedium of the present moment and the expectancy of what was to come. This was the most anxious time, as the evening drew near. Since it first happened it was difficult to concentrate, but especially in the closing moments of the working day when the anticipation grew with the sweeping hands of the clock.

He looked around furtively at his work colleagues; did they notice? Was there a change in his behaviour? They busied themselves in the illusion of the importance of their tasks but he could feel their eyes resting on him, probing, asking questions he could never answer, not because he was evasive, but because the answer was beyond his comprehension. What was happening to him was an enigma, the magnitude of which defied his rational thought. He wondered in the silence of his self imposed isolation if he was truly unique, or were there others in some remote corner of the world who had lived through the same experience, if not in his lifetime, then at some time in the past, hundreds, even thousands of years ago? It was difficult to believe that at least one other living soul had not been through the same sequence of events that were now taking over his life.

Although he had no control of the situation, he was not attempting to resist it; why should he? This inexplicable happening was the most exciting thing he had ever experienced. It felt like a blessing in answer to an unconscious prayer; he was being rescued and extracted from the mundanity of his life and into the realm of his deepest desires. But why? If it was a response to an unconscious prayer, was there a price to pay? The thought touched him with a trace of fear that tarnished the thrill and left him uneasy. This was not how life developed its complex stories. Fortune and happiness were never served up indefinitely and certainly not so liberally. There was always a cost and life always collected on its debts; one way or another. This sudden change of life events seemed too poetic, too contrived. He felt like a stooge, an unwitting victim gorging on the candy of life while those who devised the plot hid among the shadows and waited for the moment when they would end the game and demand payment. But the possibility of a price to pay was academic because he could not stop what was happening to him, even if fear, wisdom or some other latent virtue desired its end.

He closed the file in front of him and returned it to a large brown folder printed with the words, *Finch & Beckett Chartered Accountants*. Finch and Beckett were long dead and long forgotten, with the exception of the whimsical rumour that claimed their ghosts walked the corridors in the dead of night in search of a missing ledger; doomed for eternity to seek out the page that will balance the books of their life's endeavours. But beyond this, their names lived on in the accountancy firm that Simon toiled in nine hours a day, five days a week. It was said that if you were not a senior partner by the time you were thirty five, you never would be. Simon's thirty-fifth birthday came and went three years earlier and he was still not a senior partner. In fact he was not even a junior partner. After twelve years with the firm, he still languished unnoticed on the first floor, handling the client accounts that no one else wanted. The resentment mounted slowly over the years. He resented those who failed to promote him and those who were promoted over his head. He resented the clients, whose financial accounts he prepared, all of whom earned four times his own salary. In fact he resented everything that Finch and Beckett stood for, from the senior partners' opulent office suite on the fifth floor to the asthmatic whine of the photo copier next to his desk that frayed his nerves at random intervals throughout his colourless, tiresome day.

This all culminated in his assertion that his professional life had so far been a complete failure. Not only had he failed, but he had failed in a career that he now detested. The bright, affable and promising student that walked out of university had lost his way as he navigated the career path. Somewhere along the journey he fell from the golden trail of prosperity and landed in the muddy ditch of professional life and the more he struggled to climb out, the more the groping clutches of fate clawed him back into the mire. The columns of figures and pages of spreadsheets that at one time fired his enthusiasm, now merely extinguished any glimmer of light that might have brightened his day. Even the promised security that his profession offered was no longer a benefit. It was now just a chain that shackled him to a dead career; chained to the security of a monthly salary cheque; just enough to keep him in fear of losing it but woefully short of an income that would allow him to taste the varied flavours of life.

When he looked at his watch again it was twenty past five, close enough to call an end to the working day. He raced to catch the 17.46 train, but missed it and caught the slower 17.55 instead. It made little difference, for at his destination, no one waited with a heart of desire in anticipation of his homecoming.

All the seats were taken so he stood at one end of the corridor and surveyed the rows of grim faces. Each stared into an available vacant space to avoid making inadvertent eye contact with a complete stranger and when all the vacant spaces were used up they tried to become anonymous hiding under the veil of transient, fitful sleep.

He pitied them, their grey, ashen faces revealing the truth of their grey ashen lives, returning from a soul destroying job to a banal home and lacklustre life. But the pity came not from a detached observer, but from his empathy with their plight. He knew their struggle, for he was one of them; he was blighted by the same daily existence and the knowledge that tomorrow would deliver the same as today, and yet for reasons he did not understand he had been given a lifeline to something else, something that defied all the natural laws of the human experience. He was swept up by it, tantalised by it, but dared not question it for fear it may disappear as suddenly and as mysteriously as when it first entered his life.

He felt a thrill rushing through his body at the thought of what tonight might bring, and in the same moment he was struck by the worry of how he would conceal it and appear to conduct his normal life. What excuse could he find for going to bed at nine o'clock again? How many more times could he say he was extra tired or not feeling well? Rebecca was starting to notice. It was not the caring concern of a doting wife, but just another point of conflict to argue about. She did not care about what time he went to bed or whether he went to bed at all, in fact it was several years since she had even been aware of his presence in bed, but any opportunity for antagonism was seized upon.

Maybe tonight he would delay it until ten o'clock. That would be quite reasonable. It was an acceptable time to go to bed when he had to be up early for work, but it would still leave him enough time for the full uninterrupted experience of whatever was to happen.

Through the darkened windows of the train he could see the platform signs for Wessingdon Hill station, a suburban sprawl like countless others in the north of England. It manifested like all the other new suburban towns on the outskirts of the major industrialised centres in an effort to provide a respite from the noise and pollution of the city. But as the city grew, the suburbs were encroached upon and eventually consumed by the excesses of the city that it sought to evade. This was home, but only in name. Far from feeling the warmth that a home should radiate, it shared the cold isolation of his marriage and grey tedium of his job. It was a cultural wasteland, an architectural scar and a failed housing experiment conducted by town planners devoid of vision, who designed without the necessary soul to create habitation fit for a creative species. But despite this, he continued to live here and

Wessingdon Hill remained home despite it making little sense. He chose not to think too much about it, but pondered that maybe apathy breeds more apathy and the downward spiral continues until the senses are numbed enough so as not to notice.

Stepping off the train the first thing he noticed was the smell from the chemical factory. The wind was coming from the west again and brought with it the toxic vapour of the by-product of chemicals that the company said were going to make everyone's lives richer and better. He remembered the time before the chemical factory was built. He could not remember being less rich or worse off in any way at that time, but he *could* remember being able to smell the wild flowers from the meadow that no longer existed and the wood smoke from the cottages in the village; the village that was razed to the ground in order to build the chemical factory.

He turned left out of the station but did not bother to run for the bus that waited at the vandalised bus shelter amidst a carpet of shattered glass fragments. If he walked home it would take twenty five minutes instead of the ten minutes it would take on the bus, and that would expire a little more of the evening that lay ahead until he could go to bed.

It was completely dark now and with the darkness came the rain and the cold evening chill of late October. In this bleak and dispirited place the darkness was a friend, for it hid the ugliness of the warehouses and canals that framed his route home. He knew they were still there but now they were dark indiscernible shapes that huddled in the rain and with a little imagination he could transform them into great edifices with steeples and architraves and sculpted gargoyles that watched over the town. But he could not do the same with the remains of the stolen car that lay abandoned beneath the orange glow of a street light. It seemed as if it was on display, illuminated under a spotlight as a warning not to leave your car unattended at any time or for any reason. It had now been there for two weeks and each time he passed it a little more had been cannibalised. First the wheels, then the lights. the door mirrors and wipers and when there was nothing left that could be removed, the windows were smashed and bodywork daubed in graffiti by an delinquent of questionable literacy. And now it lay there, rusting and decaying, stripped of its identity, a barely recognisable shell of its former self; not unlike Wessingdon Hill itself, a town stripped of its identity; no heart, no soul, cannibalised of anything it once had that was worth having, and now an empty shell ripe for the harbouring of iniquity.

By the time he reached his front door his clothes were drenched but he was untroubled by being so wet. He stood in the doorway shaking the excess rain from his coat outside, because walking indoors with a dripping wet coat was sufficient reason for Rebecca's wrath. She walked into the hallway and saw him diligently drying off his coat, "It's pouring, didn't you wait for the bus?" she asked.

He looked around, surprised to see her standing there. For a moment he thought he detected a hint of care in her voice, then saw her expression and realised she was just concerned about his wet shoes on the carpet. There was a time when she would have driven to the station to meet him when it was raining, but that was so long ago that the mists of time obscured the memory. He could barely even remember what happened to change things so much. He looked at her as she monitored the water seeping from his shoes into the carpet in a growing plume. She was still very attractive, not in the same way as when they first met; the perception of beauty loses its lustre when the passing of time inevitably leads to familiarity. But physically she had changed little; the years had been kind to her in the same way as they can sometimes be so cruel as they mark the passage of a life's journey. But it was her inner beauty that had faded and manifested outwardly with subtle changes, such as in the way the corners of her mouth sloped downwards like an irresistible concession to gravity, and the way her eyes, which once shone so brightly, now suppressed their radiance and emitted little more than a glimmer of their former brilliance. She had relinquished the things of youth before she became old and as her spirit of inner beauty died, she reflected back in the mirror not the elegant features of a woman in graceful transition towards the middle years of life, but an image that echoed disillusionment born out of the unfulfilled dreams and hopes that at one time stretched so seductively before her. And at the same time the love that graced their early years had aged and become decrepit. It was an insidious process that gave no warning and offered no chance of recovery. It was the *Titanic syndrome;* by the time the iceberg became visible, it was too late to avoid the collision. And once the flame of love and intimacy flickered it could never again burn strong and true, and eventually an ill wind would extinguish its light for eternity.

He took off his shoes as he answered. "It wasn't raining when I started walking and I'd just missed a bus, so I decided to walk instead of waiting. The bus stop has been vandalised again, broken glass all over the place. I don't know how much worse this area can get."

She ignored his reply and continued as if they had been in the middle of a long conversation. "The headmaster phoned today. Gavin has been implicated with some boys who were caught in possession of drugs. We need to go to the school and have a meeting about his future."

"Rebecca things are difficult at the office at the moment. Can you go this time?"

"He's your son too. You need to take more of an interest."

"That's not fair. I went to the school alone last time when we were summoned about his failing grades and the knife thing."

"That's different Simon. Both of us didn't have to be there to discuss his class work. And the knife thing was all your fault anyway. Who's ever heard of buying a fifteen year old a knife?"

"You know very well it was a Swiss army penknife. It has scissors and a screwdriver and things a boy needs when he's camping. I had one when I was his age and so did my father. Is it my fault if teenagers these days can't be trusted to get through a full term without stabbing each other?"

She dismissed his defence and continued caustically, "Anyway this is about a fifteen year old boy who might be a drug dealer."

"Why do you always escalate things so dramatically? Gavin's not a drug dealer. We both know him better than that. Maybe he's been hanging out with the wrong people but it doesn't make him a dealer."

"Then just look the other way, leave it to me to sort out. If you were a stronger influence in his life he wouldn't be associating with undesirables in the first place."

Simon saw a vision of the whole evening developing in front of him. He had barely taken off his shoes and he was embroiled in a full scale argument. "I'm not discussing this now. I'll phone the headmaster in the morning and deal with it, and I'll talk to Gavin and get his side of the story, so there's nothing more to say. I'm going to bed." He walked upstairs wondering if he had unconsciously orchestrated the whole argument just so he could find a plausible reason to go to bed early. Whatever had taken place, he had achieved his goal.

He soaked for an hour in a warm bath watching the steam condense on the mirror into small drops that left zigzag trails tracing their path. Some paths were straight and simple and others complex and twisted, just like life itself he mused. Why had his own path become so complex and twisted when he had never engaged in risks or veered from convention and always followed the principle of a simple life? And what was this latest twist that scared and excited him and forced him into bed hours before midnight. He began to feel anxious. He always did as the time approached. He was not sure whether it was the fear that it may never happen again or that it *would* happen again and he had no control over it.

It was nearly half past nine. He got into bed and left the bedside lamp on, wondering if he should try to read a little. It was still early and he was not really tired enough to sleep. He picked up a book from the bedside table and started to scan it, allowing his eyes to glaze over as he went through the motions of reading without absorbing the words. His mind flowed with easy thoughts, and soft hazy memories of the last few nights drifted in and out of clarity. He felt the approach of sleep, but the anticipation triggered an adrenalin rush and he jerked suddenly out of his warm soporific state. He put the book down, turned off the lamp and settled down determinedly into the depth of his pillows. He tried to still his mind and relax his breathing and lull himself into sleep. As the minutes passed the tension in his body eased and he began to sense the moment of sleep approaching. His world became quiet and vague and began to recede to a distant place, and then just as he was on the point of losing consciousness he was wrenched back violently into the waiting world with a sound that surged through his chest and caused his heart to pound. He recognised the gruff bark of his neighbour's dog in the rear garden. It was a harsh, metallic bark that grated on the airwaves and ricocheted between the garden fences.

Simon cursed the dog and mourned the moment of sleep that had been lost. He sat up in bed and waited for the echo of the barking to fade and only when he felt certain that the dog had been taken inside the house did he slip back under the duvet. He had to be asleep before Rebecca came to bed, if not he feared it may not happen tonight. She might be a negative influence or a conflict or perhaps just the sense of her presence might discourage what might have otherwise taken place.

Silence resumed and the darkness deepened and sleep beckoned cautiously from somewhere within the encroaching night. The voices in his head that retold the events of the day became echoey and distant and signalled that he was entering the gateway of sleep and the beginning of the night journey, and as seconds turned into minutes he gently stepped off the edge of consciousness and fell helplessly into the dream world.

Chapter Two

The transition into the dream was seamless and gentle. He entered the dream with the ease of stepping across the threshold of adjoining rooms. He knew immediately it was *the* dream. It was the bright, luminous white light that suffused not only everything he saw but also everything he smelled and touched and sensed. It was a light that filled him with the spirit of life itself; its quality transcending the dark misery of his waking hours.

The Californian sun was piercing the gaps in between the white bedroom shutters and stripes of golden light painted the bedroom in geometric patterns. He leapt out of bed and opened the French windows leading to the terrace, beyond which lay the grandiose vista of the Pacific Ocean. It drifted lazily in the light of the early morning and lapped its cool azure blues in sinuous layers over the shimmering bronze sand.

The sun bathed the entire length of the beach, but the cooling ocean breeze calmed the sun's intensity making the air mild to the touch and pleasant to breath. The first hours of the day always carried a fine mist in the air from the ocean spray and he felt it tingle on his skin like an invisible gossamer hand caressing away his tension and worries, and the smile he felt forming on his lips began somewhere deep inside and radiated outwards, immersing him in a growing wave of contentment. There was often a heady aroma that hung invisibly over the terrace from the small white jasmine flowers as they entwined themselves erotically around the ornate structure of the terrace. He breathed in the scent and savoured it silently and solemnly like a spiritual awakening of the new day.

He looked back into the bedroom and saw Lara still asleep, her body draped intricately within the folds of the white satin sheets. Her dark chestnut coloured hair was tousled in waves that flowed with the contours of the pillow like a delicious turbulent sea of chocolate and cream. He crept back to the bed and knelt beside her, then suddenly felt her stir and take in a deep breath. She moved slowly with long ballerina stretches that brought her gently back into the waking world and with each movement her tresses of dark hair fell away from her face to reveal curvy dark eyelashes like soft shutters over sleepy eyes. The usual blue colour of her eyes was intensified in the direct sunlight which brought out their true opalescence with jade greens and sapphire blues that duelled with each other for dominance. When she saw him looking at her, her eyes smiled; soft and subtle at first, then deepening and spreading to her lips with the warm glow that comes with the unquestioning knowledge of intimate love. "Hello." There was a playful lilt in her voice. Without breaking eye contact she stretched an arm over the side of the bed and produced a small box wrapped in silver paper and bound with a navy blue silk ribbon bow.

"What's that?" said Simon.

"It's for you; a little commemoration and a thank you for one year of happy days and blissful nights. Now I know you probably don't remember, and I don't expect you to, but today is one year since we met. Well, come on, open it."

Simon leaned over the bed and kissed her on the lips. It was a slow, deliberate, lingering kiss, the kind that goes beyond the physical act and into that ethereal bond that is always unspoken. He studied the box, then pulled one end of the ribbon and carefully unwrapped the silver paper revealing a blue velvet box. As he lifted the lid the sun immediately lit up the small silver anchor inside. It was attached to a thin silver chain that was coiled like a rope around the anchor. "It's beautiful," he said.

Lara took it from the box and placed it around his neck. "It's fits you perfectly. Now it will always remind you that I'm yours and you're mine and nothing will ever break us apart. But I also bought it to remind you that you are the most talented marine architect on the west coast and every beautiful yacht you design and build will be blessed." Simon held the anchor between his finger and thumb and then his gaze lowered to the bed.

"I haven't embarrassed you have I?" said Lara, "I really didn't expect you to know it was our anniversary; honestly, you have so much on your mind running the business that pays for all the beautiful things in our life."

Simon shifted his gaze back to her, his expression still sombre and thoughtful. He grabbed her hand and pulled her from the bed. "Come on, quick," he said.

"Where to?"

"The lighthouse, we're going to jog to the lighthouse, come on, hurry."

"But Simon, we've had no breakfast."

"Later, come on, just throw on some jogging pants or something."

They raced down the spiral stairs and out of the house through the rear sun terrace and straight onto the beach. He was one stride ahead of her, but held her hand as they ran and stumbled in the soft mounds of sugary sand. The lighthouse was two hundred metres away, built on the apex of a steep rise that led to the cliffs that enclosed the bay.

"Simon, I can't keep up." She was laughing as she was talking and her stride became more erratic in the sand. At one point they fell, but Simon picked her up and continued the pace until they reached the point where the beach began its gentle rise. Now they slowed down, taking big exaggerated steps on the sandy hill. When they reached the path to the lighthouse, Lara fell into the sand, pulling Simon down with her. "I can't move," she said through giggling heavy breaths.

They lay still in a small depression of sand with the same sense of enchantment that city children exude when immersed in nature for the first time.

"I think we should get a dog. What do you think?" said Lara.

"If you think so."

"Yes. We should get a dog, a small one, with short legs. Dogs with short legs have to work so hard for everything. They're an inspiration, the way they face all the obstacles of life and see them as a challenge. He could be our reminder to banish defeatist thoughts if they creep up on us. But I suppose most things are a challenge to a dog with short legs, especially running on the beach, don't you think?"

"I never really thought about it. But maybe that's part of the grand design; the less you have to work with, the more life force you need to achieve the same output. If we have a small dog he could be like a ship's mascot," said Simon.

"Yes, yes, he could be a sea dog, with a little red and white spotted hanky tied around his neck, like a pirate."

"What could we call him?"

"Sea dog."

"It's not very imaginative. A sea dog called sea dog," replied Simon.

"What about Napoleon?"

"Why Napoleon?"

"Because he was small, with short legs," answered Lara. "Do you think it's true what they say about short men; that they overcompensate? I think Napoleon probably overcompensated; invading all those countries just to feed his ego. He probably had a clinically obese ego; do you think that's possible? Anyway, I don't think we'll call him Napoleon. I want a feisty dog but not one who has to prove himself every day savaging all the other dogs in the neighbourhood."

"Let's just call him sea dog then." Simon looked up and raised his hand in the air.

"Who are you waving to?" said Lara, craning her neck to look round.

"Morning Frank, can we come in?" shouted Simon to the man standing at the lighthouse entrance. The man waved them forward and Simon pulled Lara to her feet, "Come on, we can go in now."

"Simon, why are going in the lighthouse?"

"Have you ever been in one before?"

"No, but why do we want to?

He ignored the question and kept hold of her hand as they entered through the small doorway. In contrast to the warm brilliance outside, the interior of the lighthouse felt small and dank. "Ugh, it makes me shiver," said Lara. "It reminds me of my grandmother's cellar. She used to store her fruit jams in there and I had to go down and get them. I can't even look at fruit jam now without getting a shiver down my spine."

"Do you know how many steps there are to the top?" asked Simon, not waiting for an answer, "I don't know either, but Frank probably knows, he's worked here for thirty years. Okay, are you ready?"

"What? You want us to climb to the top?" said Lara, her eyes opening wide.

"Of course, that's why we're here."

"But, I'm scared of heights."

"Are you? I didn't know that."

"No neither did I, I mean I don't know if I am; I've never been to the top of a lighthouse before, so I don't really know, but what if I *am* scared and freeze and go all to pieces at the top?"

"You could be stuck forever I suppose, like that girl in the fairy tale, trapped in the top of the tower. What was her name?"

"Rapunzel," answered Lara.

"I thought she was the one who pricked her finger and fell asleep for one hundred years," said Simon.

"No, that was sleeping beauty."

"Are you sure? I thought that was Snow White?"

"Simon, what sort of confused childhood did you have? You've got all your damsels mixed up. Rapunzel let her hair down so her suitor could climb up it and rescue her. That's what you will have to do if I get stuck up there."

"I don't mind doing that, but it's probably going to make your eyes water. Now enough talk; let's go."

He grabbed her hand and led the way up the winding stone stairs. Their footsteps became short and robotic, adapting quickly to the tight circle of the spiral stairway. As they ascended further, the echoes of their steps on the stone stairs reverberated within the confined space and each step spawned a dozen echoes that collided and repeated, then faded away to the depths of the lighthouse. Beyond the halfway point hovered a curious smell, the smell of damp that hangs heavy in old buildings. The moisture had seeped into the stone and mingled with the salt in the air to create a heady, potent aroma that sealed within its scent the secrets of the passage of time within the lighthouse walls. It felt austere and darkly intimidating until gradually the smell began to fade as they reached the upper section of the tower and at the same time the atmosphere began to feel lighter, fresher and warmly inviting.

Lara's pace began to slow. "Simon, my legs are wobbly, I don't know if I can make it without a rest."

"Look, we're nearly at the top, I can see the light at the top of the stairs. Just a few more steps."

They made three more circuits and then the dark shadows of the stairway gave way to the brilliance of the white light at the end of their climb. They stood quite still at the top of the world, immersed in the magnificence of the scene that greeted them; the sweeping vista of the Pacific Ocean wrapping itself around the bay.

"Oh Simon, it's so beautiful. I can see everything. All the way down to the headland beyond the bay, and look, you can even see the curve of the earth on the horizon. Why didn't you bring me up here before?"

Simon laughed, "I knew you would like it."

Lara spoke excitedly, "It's like looking down upon the earth, the way the Greek gods did when they were sitting on Mount Olympus watching over their subjects, deciding who was going to be rewarded and who was going to have a bad day. Do you think that's how it works? The gods have their favourites and grace them with calm seas throughout their lives, while others are cast adrift into hostile waters infested with monsters?"

"Do you mean destiny?" said Simon.

"I suppose so. I mean, is everything that's going to happen to us, going to happen anyway, regardless of what we do or think?"

"I'm not sure. Sometimes I think if we lived by the law of destiny what would be the point of planning anything or thinking creatively. If everything is preordained we may as well just lie in bed and wait for it to happen. Anyway, it would be too easy for the immoral and unscrupulous to corrupt the whole idea. Every criminal and degenerate would plead immunity from prosecution on the grounds that their nefarious acts were beyond their control. Responsibility would lose its meaning; imagine you are in a restaurant and faced with the choice of the high calorie, sugary, unhealthy desert or the light fresh fruit salad, and you choose the heart attack pudding; you could happily combat the guilt by saying it was destined and the question of willpower wouldn't even be raised. No, I think it's a bit more subtle, more like a road map with a suggested route, but you are free to branch off onto the side roads as you see fit."

"That's a bit scary," said Lara, "It's like we are all alone with our free will and at the mercy of other people's free will, like those degenerates you mentioned. I feel more comfortable with the idea of the gods keeping an eye on us."

"Well maybe some of us have a god in our corner who bends the rules for us when times are hard. I suppose the trick is how to get a god on your side who's going to keep the storms and the monsters at bay."

Lara was gazing down to the beach below watching a jogger running alongside her dog. "Well I probably don't really need the protection of the gods, not as long as I have you looking out for me. However, if you and I were a couple of gods, we'd make a great job of it from up here in our lighthouse, bending all the rules to help out our favourite subjects." She switched her gaze to Simon and studied him with a deep probing look. "I wonder which god you would be? Maybe Zeus would suit you; I don't mean the beard and all the big hair, just his character. "

"Are you sure? I don't think you'd be very happy if I was Zeus." said Simon.

"Why not; wasn't he a nice god?"

Simon smiled, "He was a bit of a lothario; had lovers all over the heavens, not what you'd call a role model for fidelity or a bastion of the school of monogamy."

"Oh no, no, forget I said that. That's definitely not you: is it?" Lara said with a whiff of optimism laced in her voice. "I know; you could be Poseidon, god of the sea. That's a perfect god for a marine architect, navigating the waves, trident aloft in your hand."

"Now that's more promising; overseer of the oceans, very nautical, but he had a tendency towards belligerence; always rubbing someone up the wrong way; could lead to a stormy relationship for us."

"No, that's no good either, that's not you. I don't see you as the confrontational type. So who does that leave?"

Simon stared far out to the horizon and stroked his chin in a perfect cameo of the quintessential contemplative gesture."Well what about Apollo, god of light and music and truth; honest sort of deity, good on instruments you twang and something of a healer when he wasn't traversing the cosmos on his winged chariot."

"Yes, I like the sound of that. That's much more you and the winged chariot's a good metaphor for one of your lovely yachts. So if you're Apollo, who would I be?"

Simon paused again, "Well, Aphrodite comes to mind, goddess of beauty and love. She also had this kind of enchanted girdle that could make anyone fall for her."

"Really? That sounds a bit sinister; like entrapment. I'd want you to be in love with me without some sort of trick underwear coercing you."

"Well there's always Athena, goddess of the intellect, culture, arts, literature; they all sound like a good fit for you."

"Yes, that's more like it. I think I could pass for Athena."

"She was also a virgin goddess."

"You could have told me that first," laughed Lara.

"I've got the perfect goddess for you," Simon responded quickly, "not a Greek, but a Roman goddess. Venus; the goddess of love, feminine charisma, seduction; all those wonderful things that you are."

"Okay, that's settled. You're Apollo and I'm Venus and we'll govern the world with wisdom, justice and fairness from our Mount Olympus at the top of the lighthouse."

"The only problem is," said Simon, "we've mixed our gods, Roman and Greek. I'm not sure that would be wise. We'd be breaking the rules and distorting the established conventions of mythology."

"It's all getting confusing isn't it. My knowledge of Greek mythology is worse than your knowledge of fairy tales. I don't think we should be gods after all. Let's just leave people to sort it out themselves and run their own lives and we can just watch the world go by from up here instead." Lara looked back towards the beach. "Look, there's our house. It seems so lost on this enormous beach. Do you think it's lonely? I don't think it is. I think it's happy, don't you think so? It looks like its smiling. I never knew houses could smile."

"Oh yes, it's common knowledge that houses can smile, they just need a reason. Houses are like people. They can be jubilant or dark, affluent or in poverty, they have halcyon days and sombre times and eventually they grow old and one day they will die, and if they were loved and cherished, tears will fall for them. Our house is always smiling these days, but you see the third house along, the one with the blue roof? That one isn't smiling. It's a sad house that wears a frown. The door is shut tight like lips that won't speak and the windows sag, like defeated eyes that don't want to look onto the world anymore."

"Do you know who lives there?"asked Lara.

"I used to know them. They've gone now: two ordinary people who fell out of love with life and each other and just waited for something to come along and change things for them, but it never did. Nothing ever just comes along. *They* had a dog, a small black and white terrier, barked incessantly; then one day he just stopped and never barked again. I think he gave up too." Simon suddenly turned around and looked at the light in the centre of the lighthouse. "Do you know how bright the light in a lighthouse needs to be?"

"Simon you're like an excited schoolboy with your questions; how many steps are there, how bright is the light? Do you want to slide down the banister on the way down too?"

"No seriously, that light has to shine out to sea for miles. It has to penetrate the darkest nights and the heavy sea mists that we get here. No ordinary light can do that."

"Well if you really want to know, you can always ask Frank," she said.

"No I don't need to, I already know. All lighthouses are powered by a single diamond. It's the only way to create such a powerful, permanent light."

Lara laughed, "Don't be silly, they don't have diamonds in lighthouses. It would cost a fortune."

"They do, I'm not kidding. Have a look into the light; see if you can see the diamond."

Lara turned and looked into the light, still laughing at the absurd idea of diamond powered lighthouses. Then suddenly she stopped, stunned and silent. Her eyes opened wide and she started to shake as her heart thumped heavily. Simon looked at her, then turned towards the light. "You see, I told you, I can see the diamond from here. That's strange though, it seems to be attached to something. It's a ring isn't it?" He reached out and picked up the diamond ring from in front of the light. The precious stone ricocheted light from every angle in bursts of spectral colours and the hues made complex patterns that danced chaotically."Shall we see if it fits you?" He slipped the ring onto her finger and with a more solemn tone in his voice, he said, "Yes, actually I did remember that today is one year since we met and I was thinking that that is more than enough time to know that I want to marry you and spend the rest of my life with you. So perched up here in the sky, half way to the moon and with the Pacific as our witness, what do you think? Are you prepared to risk it?"

Lara tried to speak, her lips quivered but no words escaped. A thousand words formed in her mind, each jumbled and in disarray and incapable of forming one coherent sentence that was befitting of the intensity of the moment. As seconds passed she gave up trying and allowed the tears that streamed from her eyes to speak for her. She threw arms around him and wept in silence at the top of the world, just the two of them, alone with the Pacific Ocean.

"Congratulations." The voice came from Frank, the lighthouse keeper who waved with a knowing smile as they both tumbled down the sandy bank back to the beach. They walked back to the house, slowly and in silence, Lara glancing at the ring on her finger every few seconds. As they stepped onto their terrace Lara looked down the beach to the third house along, the sad one with the blue roof. "Simon, those people who lived in the sad house, you don't think we'll ever become like them do you?"

"Why are you thinking that way?"

"Don't you ever get frightened when you feel so happy and everything is going so well?"

"Look at this house," he said, "our house. I designed it from the ground up. There's not a single frown in it. The whole house exudes confidence, it's filled with curves that smile and doorways that welcome. I didn't know you at the time, but I know I designed it with you in mind. I built it around you, though we were yet to meet. That's the confidence I had, the confidence that I built into the house. It will take care of us and everything will work out because it's meant to be that way. Now; I distinctly remember you mentioning breakfast."

They walked into the kitchen and Lara began slicing fruit for the electric blender. "I'm just going to have a quick shower," said Simon. He turned on the shower taps and waited for the water to warm up, but something troubled him. It was the sound of the electric blender. It sounded strange, not the usual smooth buzz, but more of a shrill, grating sound. He called out to the kitchen, "Lara, is the blender okay? It sounds weird." There was no reply, but the blender started to sound even stranger and then louder. He felt agitated, unnerved by something. The shower water was still cold and then the blender started to sound like a drill, but the sound was not coming from the kitchen. It was as if it was in his head, gyrating inside his skull like a frantic bee in the final death throes of late summer. And then it became dark, and then darker still until all was black and he slipped back across the threshold from the dream world into his own existence. But it was not the same smooth transition as when he entered the dream: now he was torn away, wrenched from the joy of his sunlit dream world and plunged back into the dark despair of his life. His eyes were still closed, but the strange sound of the electric blender that buzzed in his head now revealed itself. It transformed into the alarm clock that buzzed aggressively on the bedside table. He stretched out an arm, his eyes still closed and fumbled to find the clock, eventually bringing down his fist onto it and rendering it silent.

Chapter Three

As the seconds passed and reality returned he felt the suffocating raw depression of his existence descend over him. It was always the same in the immediate moments following the dream, the stark contrast was graphic and cruel and malicious. There was a period of shock, then disbelief, and finally reluctant acceptance of his truth.

The sense of excitement and anticipation that surged through his veins in the hours before sleep now became a heavy burden laced with the bitterness of anti climax. It blighted his spirit and imprisoned his will, draining the life from his tortured being. The only light was the knowledge of the dream and its return when sleep next comes. But there too lay fear, the fear of the unknown, the fear of what was happening to him, but perhaps even greater was the fear that the dream would desert him, to disappear without trace as swiftly and as mysteriously as when it first appeared.

A small chink in the curtains revealed the first tentative light of the day. It was a grey, reluctant light, uninspiring and promising little more than the pale wash of a leaden, overcast sky. He looked across to Rebecca on the other side of the bed. She lay as far away as it was possible to be, a wide chasm that perfectly symbolised the distance that grew between them in their physical world. He crept out of bed trying not to wake her. It was the surest way to avoid an argument.

It was five past six. If he left soon he could get an earlier train and have a chance of getting a seat. If he was comfortable, there was a chance he could fall asleep, even for half an hour and if the sleep was deep enough, he would return to the dream. He rushed breakfast and left the house arriving at the station in time for the 06.50 train. The train was full. He forced his way through the carriages, surveying right and left for an empty seat. In the last carriage there was one seat free, next to the toilet. He sat down and furtively inspected his fellow passengers. Three had phones in their hands, not a promising sign for a quiet journey. There were no children, so at least he would not be assaulted by mindless, inane gibberish, although those with the mobile phones might shortly change that.

He closed his eyes and tried to focus on the dark inner curtains of his eyelids. The train eased into its rhythmic beat, numbing the mind with hypnotic patterns of muffled sounds. He had a feeling of lightness, of floating, of teetering on the edge of consciousness and just as he began to fall, the inevitable happened. The first mobile phone rang. Simon jumped, the phone startling him back to full consciousness. He was seconds from entering the dream, but now he was wide awake. He glared at the man with the phone and felt his pulse rising. Gone was the warm, soporific state and the hope of a few stolen minutes in his dream world. Now he was filled with frustration and anger and a desperate sense of how little control he had over the events of his life.

The offices of Finch & Beckett had a shabby, run down appearance from the outside. In fact only marginally less shabby than the inside. The building sat on the edge of a 1970s industrial estate adorned with the bland, unemotional and architecturally incontinent square characteristics of the period. It was a grey block, with a grey car park on a grey industrial estate and it assailed Simon's senses and stifled his life force every time he approached it. The sun never seemed to shine on this little patch of God's earth, although it must have shone at some time, but maybe it seemed too incongruous and he mentally filtered it out.

Some days were worse than others. On the worst days he felt like a condemned man making the final, long and lonely walk to the gallows. In fact, on reflection those were not the worst days; at least the walk to the gallows had a finality and an expectation of the end of the suffering. On other days he just felt as if he was in a walking coma, devoid of feeling, deaf and blind to the world and carrying out his programmed role. The best days were those when a strange rebellious nature consumed him. It was so out of character, so alien to the married, father of two, accountant. On these days the feeling drifted between complete apathy at one end to total revolution at the other, but both feelings were tinged with the sweet absence of responsibility; they unshackled him and set his spirit free to enter the world and make love or wage war or simply refuse to be a part of a system that told him what thoughts to think. But those were rare days and never consistent and most of the time he walked in a coma or trekked the lonely path to the gallows.

Today felt like a coma day. As he entered the building he saw his boss walking towards him. "Ah Simon, you're in early this morning."

"Yes, I got an earlier train."

"I'm glad I ran into you. Have you got a few minutes, I wanted to have a word. We can talk in my office."

Simon followed him to the third floor with an ominous sense of something indefinable, but not altogether pleasant. He felt as if his *coma day* was turning into a *walk to the gallows day*.

"Pull up a chair, Simon." He flopped into the least worn chair, which was actually very worn and way beyond re-upholstering, and then he looked around the office with strangely envious eyes. It was a shabby square box with a window that looked onto the delivery bay and the recycling bins. It was typical of a middle management office at Finch & Beckett; small, faceless, ubiquitously grey, but it should have been *his* office a long time ago. In fact he felt he should have been in this office many years ago and now should have moved on to the partners' suites on the fifth floor.

"The thing is Simon, you've worked here for a while now and I know about the rumours. I know they say you should have moved up the ladder a long time ago, but it's no reflection on you necessarily, it's just circumstance, do you know what I mean?"

"Is that what you wanted to talk about?" said Simon robotically.

"No, no. Well in a sense, yes, it's all part of the bigger picture. You see we like to think morale is high here at Finch & Beckett. We want people to be happy and the thing is, well, people have noticed that you seem distracted lately."

"People?" said Simon, not trying to disguise the accusation in his voice.

"Well, as I said, rumours abound in companies like ours. Someone says something to someone else and they repeat it and before long, no one knows who said what. But the fact is something was said and what I'm hearing is that things are slipping in your department and it seems like your mind isn't on your work."

Simon sat up in his chair, "Is this an official reprimand?"

"Simon, Simon, I just wanted a word with you, completely unofficial and off the record. No one has complained about you and nothing major has happened. Look, I'm just saying we all go through bad patches. We can't all give one hundred percent all the time. I'm your manager; it's my responsibility to take an interest in your welfare. I'd rather catch any problems before they happen than try to clean up after the event. I just want to help with your happiness."

Simon stared at the floor, seemingly oblivious to what had just been said. After what seemed like almost a full minute he sat upright in the chair, his eyebrows narrowed and sloping, but nothing more given away in his expression. He took in a deep breath, then spoke in a slow deliberate voice. "You're asking if you can help with my happiness Tom. Is that it? Well at the risk of offending you and blowing any glimmer of a chance of career advancement, I think you are exceeding your brief. The fact is you can't deliver what I need for my happiness. Shall I be really frank? What do you think would make me happy? Do you think it would have been having your job, about five years ago? I should have been in middle management a long time ago. I should have been doing your job. But now I should have moved on to a senior position. You're a few years older than me Tom, so you should have moved up the ladder long ago too. So what does that say about us? We're both a couple of mediocre, non starters, biding our time, waiting for the company pension to kick in. But I can't honestly answer your question because I don't know what you mean by happiness. Do you mean a full partnership and a suite on the fifth floor? A top of the range BMW in the car park, the key to the hospitality drinks cupboard and ten days a year in the company villa in Grand Cayman. But maybe I'm aiming too low, those are just material things. How about a company mistress at weekends with an expense account to furnish her needs? I hear rumours too and we both know who I'm talking about. Can you help me with that kind of happiness Tom? But maybe that's not the kind of happiness you had in mind. Maybe it's not about salary packages with early pensions and a health scheme. Maybe it's something you will never understand because your responsibilities to me have nothing to do with my happiness. Your responsibilities are to do with me achieving your targets, with profit and loss, with company goals and keeping the directors off your back. So thank you for the offer, but I don't need your help with my happiness. If there is a problem with my work, then take me to task or fire me, but don't try to patronise me and play the role of some kind of great guru of inner peace and happiness who can fill me with joy with his infinite wisdom and experience. Now if you have nothing more to say, I have to start my work before someone starts complaining about me." He stood up, maintaining eye contact just long enough to reinforce his outburst without inviting further confrontation. He turned and left the office briskly leaving Tom stunned into an uncomfortable silence and bristling with the sting of Simon's verbal assault. As he walked down the corridor he realised this was neither a *coma day* nor a *gallows walk day*: it had turned into a full blown, *take no prisoners, rebellious* day, and it felt good. Maybe he would be out of a job before the end of the day but would that be such a bad thing? How much worse would life have to get before desperation instigated something that might save him?

At his desk he brushed away the pile of papers that concealed his phone and dialled an extension. "Hello, Damien? It's Simon. Do you have any plans for lunch? I really need to talk to you about something."

"I wasn't planning on having a long lunch today Simon, I've got so much on....."

"It's really important. I wouldn't ask if it wasn't urgent."

"Is anything wrong?"

"Well, I might have just managed to get myself fired, but that's not what I want to talk about. It's something more important, can we meet at lunchtime, even for half an hour?"

"Yes, okay, of course. I'll see you outside at half past one."

The morning drifted by in a haze of tedium and trivial distractions that interrupted the flow of Simon's thoughts. He knew exactly what he wanted to tell Damien, but struggled to know *how* to tell him without it sounding like he was losing his mind. Maybe he *was* losing his mind? That would make everything so simple and explicable. He could retire to a nice institution somewhere in the country with white padded walls and minimum security gates at the end of a gravel drive. He could spend his life alternating between lying in bed and reclining on a bench under a willow tree, liberally dosed with drugs designed to help him keep a tentative toe in the external reality while living his own internal reality in the vast fantasy universe of his mind. And who was to say that that was an abnormal life? Who could categorically state that those poor wretched souls who were clinically diagnosed, labelled as mentally unfit and perpetually sedated were not living a truer, more authentic reality than those in the external world, for is it not the external world where mankind foolishly believes he can seek out the elusive answer that will satisfy all his desires? Where he can feed his lust for wealth and power, where he can acquire and accumulate possessions; houses and more houses and bigger houses and more cars and more people, but in particular one special person, one person to own and possess so the vices of coveting and jealousy and games of control can be played out with that one special person and perfected over years. And after decades and centuries and millennia of lifetimes, mankind still seeks happiness and truth and lasting peace in these possessions of the external world, though they falter and fail and fail again. So is it so preposterous to suggest that those labelled as insane or teetering on the fringe of insanity are the ones who have found peace and contentment in their own internal world, freed from the false necessities and fabricated desires of the external world?

If he were to be clinically labelled as suffering from some form of mental aberration, what difference would it make? It would not change his experience, regardless of what a man in a white coat with letters after his name might call it.

It was almost half past one. He grabbed his coat and hurried outside. Damien was waiting close to the entrance, upwind of the clique of smokers who huddled in small circles as if to disguise the act forced upon them by their addiction. Although it was never officially stated, smoking was tantamount to subversion in the eyes of Finch & Beckett. It required several minutes a day away from the office: so, on one notable Monday morning, someone from the fifth floor, in the best traditions of accountancy calculated the total production minutes lost per year through smoking. The shocking result revealed that each smoking employee was taking the equivalent of an extra seven and a half days per year in unofficial paid leave. But the company was powerless to do anything to change it except for making it known through the reliable channels of rumour that it took a dim view of excessive time away from the work desk for the purpose of feeding a nicotine addiction. So the smokers continued to smoke, huddled together in ever tighter circles in the hope of avoiding positive identification. Non smoking onlookers always assumed smoking was a social experience, because smokers always appeared outside office buildings in groups, but the truth was, they were merely adopting the policy used successfully by large shoals of fish, where the bigger the group, the less chance a single individual had of being targeted.

Simon weaved through the groups, unconsciously holding his breath to avoid the smoke. It was years since he had stopped smoking and there was little chance of him reverting to his old habit again, but he always played safe and avoided the risk of temptation. "Damien, thanks for meeting me."

"Simon, what's going on? Are you in trouble?"

"Not here, I want to get away from the office. Let's go to the cafe by the canal, it's quiet there."

They found a table close to the edge of the canal and ordered sandwiches and coffee. Damien took a pack of cigarettes from his pocket, then returned it again, not wishing to smoke in Simon's presence. "That's okay," said Simon, "smoke if you want to, I'm fine with it."

"No you're not," said Damien, "I know how you avoid it and I'm not going to be responsible for you starting again. So, what's going on? How have you managed to get yourself in a position to be fired?"

"Well, I haven't; or maybe I have; I don't really know. Tom saw me as I was coming in this morning and started with one of his fake pep talks. He was actually trying to reprimand me, but didn't have guts to do it properly. I don't know what happened, I just launched into him, not aggressively, but I think it would have come across as being pretty offensive; anyway it wasn't a glowing example of interpersonal skills in the workplace, especially to your boss. But I honestly don't care too much. If he thinks I overstepped the mark and fires me I'll let him have my full uncensored thoughts with both barrels, then thank him and walk away, never to return. But there are bigger issues that are troubling me; that's what I want to talk to you about."

"Okay, I'm listening."

"How long have we known each other Damien?"

"Are you seriously asking me that question? Because if you are, you're going to make me nervous. Whenever that question comes up between two people who have known each other forever, it means some kind of bombshell is about to be dropped. The person you thought you knew is someone completely different. How bad is it? Are you embezzling the company or into some kind of industrial espionage? You're not sleeping with one of the senior partners' wives are you? – No, no, I've seen them all, you definitely wouldn't be doing that".

"Come on Damien, be serious, this is important."

Damien suppressed the smile and adopted a more neutral expression. "Okay, how long have we known each other? Well, we met at sixth form college, then went to the same university and finally managed to end up in the same firm of accountants, so with a few breaks in between we've been around each other for over twenty years I suppose."

Simon paused briefly, seemingly in deep thought, then he spoke again, his expression intense and solemn. "And in that time, would you say I was rational and level headed."

The smile returned to Damien and developed into a soft laugh, "Are you kidding? Rational and level headed? Simon you are an accountant. You've worked in the same stuffy, conservative company for most of your professional life, you have two weeks holiday a year in the same hotel in the same Italian resort, you have life insurance and an inflation linked pension and you carry a telescopic umbrella in your bag for ten months of the year. I think most people would call that rational and level headed and I think you know that too, so why are you asking?"

"Because I need to hear someone else say it, someone who knows me well and can judge the situation objectively."

"What situation?"

Simon looked around unconsciously, ensuring no one was within hearing distance before he spoke again. "This is going to sound completely insane, but please just let me finish. The first time it happened was about five weeks ago. It was when I had those few days off from work with that terrible virus that everyone was getting. I'd been at home for two days feeling really lousy and tired. I went to bed really early, about nine in the evening and fell into a deep sleep. And that's when it happened." He stopped talking and stared into nowhere in particular.

Damien's eyes narrowed and the smile had completely gone. "What happened?" he said.

Simon continued, "It was the first time I had the dream. It's me, but I am a completely different person. I live in America, on the west coast, living in a huge luxury beach house overlooking the Pacific Ocean. In the dream I am a marine architect. I design and build these enormous ocean-going yachts and people come to me from all over the world to create their dream yacht. I have a large successful business turning over millions. My own personal wealth ensures I am extremely comfortable and surrounded by all the trappings of luxury. Life is wonderful; in fact it's perfect, perfect the way real life never is. Then I met someone and fell completely in love, more totally in love than I could ever have imagined would be possible. Her name is Lara, she's tall and slim and tanned with long dark hair and green eyes; she has a heart of pure gold, speaks three languages fluently and thinks I was sent from heaven to be with her." He stopped and stared at the clouds.

"Sounds a really good dream to me," said Damien, "I only dream of missing trains and losing my teeth and endless columns of figures that don't add up. I wish I could have dreams like yours. But I don't see where the problem is."

Simon continued. "I woke up from the dream with a great feeling, a sense of happiness and excitement. Even though I was ill, I started to feel so much better. It was like being drunk, but without the headache and dizziness. The feeling stayed with me all day. It showed me a life that I could have had if things had been different. That night I went to bed early again; all the remedies I was taking made me feel so drowsy, so I fell asleep quickly. Then I entered the dream again, just like the night before. I was in the beach house drinking coffee and looking out to the ocean. Lara was sitting on my lap sharing my coffee."

Damien started to laugh, "Simon that's nothing to worry about. Recurring dreams are very common. Lots of people have them at some time in their life. Usually they're just insights or messages telling us to be aware of something we need to deal with. My dream about the columns of figures that don't add up has been with me for years, but it doesn't bother me and even if it did...."

Simon stopped him abruptly, "No, this isn't a recurring dream. That's just the problem. If it was a recurring dream it would make complete sense and it wouldn't bother me. But it's not recurring. It's a continuation. Since the first dream five weeks ago, I have been back into the dream every night and in the last two weeks I have even been able to enter it if I fall asleep on the train or while reading a book in a chair at the weekend. But the dream progresses, it moves forward from where it left off the previous time. It's like being in a soap on TV where the story develops and life goes forward. Last night in the dream I proposed to Lara. We were in a lighthouse and I put a diamond ring on her finger. She said yes and cried. Today is the first anniversary of our time together. She gave me a silver ship's anchor pendant to commemorate it." He put his hand to his neck unconsciously to feel for it, then felt a little foolish as he became conscious of what he had done. He withdrew his hand quickly and said to Damien, "Tell me honestly; what do you make of it, with what I've told you so far."

Damien looked away from him for a moment, his expression offering no clues to his thoughts or assumptions. He looked back at Simon and spoke sympathetically, but without attempting to disguise the firmness in his voice. "You can probably imagine how this sounds to someone who is not having the same experience as you. I don't doubt you are having it, but I do have doubts as to exactly *what* it is you are having. I'm trying not to be sceptical, but I have never heard of someone having a dream of this kind without it being a conventional recurring dream. I can't even begin to understand it; you don't understand it yourself, but how could you, there's no known record of this kind of phenomena, at least not as far as I'm aware. Look Simon, the mind plays funny tricks in dreams. Sometimes recurring dreams don't feel like they're recurring. By the time you wake up, it all feels different."

"You don't believe me?"

"It's not a question of belief, I already said I'm sure you really are experiencing what you described, but we don't know what that is. Anyway I don't think it's something you need to be worried about. But you asked what I thought about what you had told me so far. What else is there?"

Simon was about to speak when a waitress approached the table with their sandwiches and coffee. He motioned to Damien to wait until she had gone. As she laid the table he fidgeted nervously with the napkin and looked around furtively, shifting his gaze erratically the way people do when trying not to look conspicuous but only succeeding in drawing more attention to themselves. The waitress smiled and walked away. Damien waited until she was far enough away not to hear before he spoke, "Was that your idea of looking nonchalant? The way you acted, that girl probably thought you really were an industrial spy."

Simon ignored his comments and continued from where he left off. "I called it a dream. That's the only way I can think to describe it which makes it vaguely understandable. But it's more than a dream. As the weeks have passed and this other life has developed by way of my dream, I am starting to wonder which is the true reality. I can't be sure anymore. I feel I could be sitting here at this table with you now, but this is actually a dream. How do I know you are real, or the girl who brought the lunch or my outburst at Tom this morning? All of this feels so unreal, but my other life, the beach house, the successful business,

Lara, the woman I am in love with, in fact the only woman I have ever been in love with; that feels real; that's where I belong, it's the only time that I feel truly happy and at peace."

Damien swallowed the piece of sandwich he was chewing hastily and spoke in a confident, matter of fact tone, "I can't vouch for you, but I assure you I am real, one hundred percent flesh and bone."

"But so is Lara; she's as real to see and touch as you are now. So which one is the dream? The truth is Damien, if Lara and my American life is just a dream and one day it just stops happening, I don't know what I will do. Since it began, I realised it was my only reason for living. I felt like a blind man seeing for the first time. Once I had tasted a different way of life I knew I could never go back, I could never again live without the life I have found and most of all I could never live without Lara. That is where my reality lies. But if that whole life is just my imagination, then this can only be the start of a mental breakdown and I'm about to lose my mind.

Damien put his coffee cup down and pushed his half empty plate to one side. "Simon, this woman, Lara; she does not exist. She is only in your head. You created her. The beach house, the boats, the money in the bank, they are all in your head, all created by your imagination and projected through your dreams. I can't begin to explain the nightly progression of your dream and I won't even try, but you have to come to terms with who you are and more importantly, where you are. Look Simon, I've already said we go back a long way. You're more like my brother. I'm family, I think I know you better than your own wife and kids know you, so let me speak to you the way only someone who is that close to you can. This might sound blunt and it might even offend you, but I hope it doesn't. I'm only saying this because I'm looking out for you and want to help you. Who else have you talked to about this?"

"No one, only you. You're the only person I could trust."

"Okay, that's good that no one else knows. My honest feeling is that I'm surprised something like this had not happened sooner. Just look at your life. You're married to a woman who you barely talk to except for when you are arguing. You've never said it to me explicitly, but from what you *have* told me, there is no love in your marriage, but that doesn't surprise me either. When I was your best man and we stood at the front of the church waiting for Rebecca to walk down the aisle, I was praying that something would happen to stop the wedding. I wanted her to trip and twist an ankle or for the church roof to leak or for you to get appendicitis or something, anything just to give me a few more days to try to talk you out of it. I've always felt guilty that I didn't do something earlier to stop you going ahead with the marriage. I knew; we both knew that she was not the one for you, but the whole wedding seemed to have a power of its own and before you could see sense, it was all over and done. I don't think I have ever seen you truly happy with Rebecca. But then there are your kids. I'm sorry mate, but you have to admit they're not god's gift to parents. It's not you, I've watched you do everything to bring them up the best way you can; that private education must be costing you a fortune, but some kids are just trouble from the outset. Please don't be offended Simon, I wouldn't be saying this if I didn't care."

Simon was staring into the sky again. He hadn't touched his food but he looked back to Damien when he heard the silence, "No, no I'm not offended, everything you say is true."

Damien continued again quickly, "But that's not all Simon. Your personal life is in crisis, but your professional life is no better. I know you hate your job and now you've got management on your back. I'm not surprised your mind's not on your work anymore. But you hate the job anyway. I saw you lose your interest after being passed over for promotion, but that was a few years ago and nothing has changed. I honestly don't know how you can make ends meet financially, what with that huge mortgage you took out and keeping two kids in private education. It's incredible that you can make your salary stretch that far."

"Well, the fact is I can't. Every month the debt rises."

"You know, when I joked about you embezzling the company funds, it was only a half joke. Just for a moment I thought this meeting and all the secrecy was a confession, or an offer to split the proceeds with me; but it was only for a second, I knew that wasn't you; not honest conventional Simon." He was silent for a moment, then his expression changed to a more sombre one. "Look Simon, the suggestion you made about this being the onset of a nervous breakdown sounds the most likely explanation to me and it's the one thing I want you to avoid at all cost. It was only a matter of time before something like this happened. It's the body's way of telling you all is not well and you need to sit up and pay attention and act before it's too late. You've just had this little exchange with Tom. Why not go and tell him you are under pressure and you need some time away, two, three weeks maybe. He'll listen to you. It's perfect timing because it will justify and mitigate what happened between you this morning. Tell him you need to get away."

"Gardening leave?" said Simon, "isn't that what they call it? Paid leave for the unstable."

"The idea is to give you the time out so you *don't* become unstable. My god, one of the senior partners had four weeks *gardening leave* last year and he came back like he was on fire, sacked three senior managers, closed down a whole department and was awarded a ten per cent pay rise, so don't dismiss it. Take the time and get away. Go abroad, somewhere hot with a beach and nothing else to do. Go alone. Tell Rebecca you need the time alone. Then come back and decide what to do about your marriage. Either work to save it or end it and move on. You won't be the first. Then you can start thinking about your job; don't sit around waiting for a promotion that may never come. There are other firms out there always looking for people."

"Yeah, looking for young hotshots, skilled, talented people full of zest and ambition. What do I have to offer? Someone heading swiftly towards middle age who has spent too long in one of the less fashionable accountancy firms, ignored for a promotion and struggling with a dysfunctional home life. Yeah I'm sure they'll all be fighting over snapping me up."

Damien shook his head irritably, "That's not the way it is and you know it. You're just in a rough stage of life and everything looks hopeless, but do what I say; get away from everything here for a while and you will have a new state of mind that will enable you to make changes."

"You make it sound easy Damien; that's not a criticism and if this is all in my head, as you think it is, well it all makes good sense. But what if it's not my imagination? What if I've tapped into something that neither of us can explain? What then?"

Damien picked up the last remnant of his sandwich and studied it absently, his mind visibly searching with a growing sense of futility, "Then I'm out of my depth. I can do the rational and the logical, but the metaphysical has never been my strong point. I want to help you Simon, I want to help you more than anything, but you need to come down to earth and let this go. If you don't, it will destroy you. Think about it; please. Let's talk again once you've had time to think about what I've said."

The afternoon was no more productive than the morning had been. Simon sat at his desk and his conversation with Damien cycled through his mind endlessly. It balanced on a see-saw, tipping between rational explanation in the form of a stress laden life, and a more exotic interpretation with a firm foundation in the realm of the metaphysical. He realised the conflict was achieving nothing and decided to leave work early, saying he was feeling unwell and to go in search of answers of his own.

Just after three o'clock he took the train into town and found an internet cafe. It was quiet and dimly lit which made him feel secure enough to delve into the depths of his mysterious condition anonymously. He sat at a terminal in the corner and entered a few search terms ranging from dreams and hallucinations to mental disorders and parallel worlds. After thirty minutes, the computer requested more money and he came to the conclusion that he was now more confused than before he began searching. He fed more coins into the machine and narrowed down his searches. He started reading about biochemical imbalances in the brain and how they could result in a range of conditions, the symptoms of which manifested as some of his own experiences. An article on forms of dementia engrossed him, particularly how it was possible for a person suffering from one particular form to mentally live in two different places and time zones. But as he read more he realised this could not be his problem because someone with that condition would be using their own selective memory to create the different time zones and places, and his dream experience of his life in America was not based on his memories. He had never even been to America and knew nothing about yachts. And most importantly his experience came only during a dreaming phase, never while he was awake. But the biochemical malfunction possibility was compelling and if nothing else, it offered the potential of labelling what he was going through and made him feel less of a unique freak of nature and more of a man with a human problem that had a scientific cause.

His eyes were hurting with such intense reading on the screen. He stopped and looked at his watch. It was quarter past five. He decided to leave so he could arrive home at about the normal time. The last thing he wanted was to have to explain to Rebecca where he had been if he was late.

He felt a strange calming satisfaction on the train journey home. The research on the internet had not resolved anything but he did not feel so alone anymore. He had told Damien everything, which had an unburdening effect and this left him open to the possibility that he was just suffering from a human condition; a condition that could be cured. It was no different to a virus or a broken leg or a throat infection, it was just that his problem was rooted in his mind. But with this feeling came also a wave of sadness. Normally at this time of the day he would feel the excitement mounting as he anticipated going to bed and falling into the dream. Lara still felt as real as the people sitting next to him on the train, but the conversation with Damien and the afternoon's research suggested otherwise and the suggestion could not be ignored. But he was still in love. He felt all the emotion of being in love, the pain, the joy, the apprehension, the only difference was that the object of his love existed within the confines of his mind or in a dream or in some other dimension that he could not explain, but she was not tangible at this moment as he sat on the 17.55 Wessingdon Hill train. And that compounded what was already an impossible situation. How could he be deeply in love with what might be no more than an apparition born out of a rogue hormone or the shadow of an unconscious desire to find his soul mate? And this revelation set off a whole new train of thought. Could it be that the dreams were prophetic? Was he experiencing through the dimension of his dreams a projection of a future that awaited him? Was it so unrealistic to believe that Lara was the dream world's embodiment of the woman that he was destined to meet? Dreams of prophecy were not outlandish, they were a foundation of modern civilised society; they were accepted and respected by scholars and theologians and men of science. Maybe Lara was not real, but the vision she represented may well be in the times to come. And suddenly the excitement revisited him and his nerves jangled with a pleasant vibration that promised of a better way of being. He felt a contentment that grew from a more plausible foundation, not one buried in pure fantasy and dreams but one that was embraced by the reality of his future. He was still in love, he still felt it, he had seen her in his dream and she was just waiting to make her presence known in his waking world.

It started to rain just before he arrived home. Damien was wrong about Simon's obsession for carrying a telescopic umbrella, for today he was without one. He ran the last few metres, but still managed to get wet enough to have to shake his coat violently in the doorway to avoid dripping onto the hall carpet. Rebecca was in the kitchen and the smell of frying onions laid a trail out into the hall. Simon took off his shoes and was about to walk upstairs to change his clothes when she appeared in the hallway carrying a wooden spoon that still smoked with rising wisps of steam. "Did you speak to him?" She used that unequivocal tone that hinted that she already knew the answer, but asked with the sole purpose of inflicting guilt or defensiveness or some other negative emotion designed to destabilise. Simon stopped at the foot of the stairs, his mind blank, her question seeming abstract and accusing. And then as he felt her stare burning into him, his mind opened like a fractured dam and her question and the implications of his answer gushed forward in an unstoppable torrent.

He sighed heavily as he answered, "The headmaster. Rebecca, it completely went out of my head. I planned to call him first thing as I got to the office, but then Tom jumped on my back before I even got my coat off. I had a lousy day and it completely slipped my mind. I will call tomorrow first thing."

"Well you needn't bother. I knew you didn't call. Do you know how I knew?" she did not wait for his reply, "I knew because the headmaster called here. Since his last call, Gavin was found in possession of what the headmaster called 'illegal substances'. They are having an enquiry and he could be suspended from school."

"Well there's nothing we can do for the moment. I'll phone Gavin. I can't believe he would be involved in drugs and I'm not going to make any judgements until I've had the chance to talk to him properly. I never had a good feeling about that school."

Rebecca waved the wooden spoon in the air as she spoke, the steam still rising from it giving her the comical impression of a pantomime witch in a camp performance of casting a spell, but Simon had little appetite for seeing the humour and Rebecca as ever was far from joviality, "So it's the schools fault that our son is under the threat of suspension for drug trafficking."

"Don't be ridiculous, it's not drug trafficking and it was you who insisted that we send him away to that public school in the first place. Do you know how much it costs per term? He could have gone to a state school and got involved with drugs for free."

"So now it's my fault for choosing the school is it; never your fault, always someone else's responsibility."

"Look Rebecca, it's no one's fault, not yours, not mine, not the schools. We don't know the facts yet, let's wait until we've both spoken to Gavin and then we can start talking about blame if we want to."

"Well now that you've mentioned the school fees, there's a letter from the bank. Last month's fee took us over our overdraft limit again. They say that's the fourth time in the last six months and they want to talk to you about it. So that's another call you can forget to make tomorrow."

Simon ignored her and began walking wearily up the stairs, but stopped half way as he heard Rebecca's voice again. "Just in case you disappear into the bedroom for the rest of the night, you might be wondering where your daughter is again for the second night in a row."

"No, why would I be wondering, you already told me she's staying at her friend's house for the week."

"Well what you don't know and what I found out today is that her friend has a nineteen year old brother who has suddenly declared his love for her and I'm not sure if Mandy is spending the week at her friend's house to be with her friend or to be with the nineteen year old brother."

"Nineteen? Mandy's only just thirteen, she can't fall in love with a nineteen year old."

"Well you need to tell her that, but she might disagree. Maybe you could make a note to talk to her when she's back, after you've spoken to Gavin and the bank if you're not too busy. It's turning into quite a hectic schedule for you."

Simon ignored her and continued up the stairs without looking back. Rebecca had sharpened the sting of her sarcasm over the years, honing it to a cutting edge that would have mercilessly lacerated the fibre of his emotions had he not learned to ignore her jibes and allow them to fall on ears that ceased to listen.

He stared out from the bedroom window and watched the plumes of smoke that drifted from the chemical factory. The white smoke reflected the orange glow from the street lighting and it hung in the atmosphere like a radioactive cloud reminding him of the ugliness that embodied his personal world. He was desperate for Lara; she could soothe him now and dissolve his desperation. She could erase the ugliness and squalor from his life and bathe him in beauty and light and the warmth that a soul craves in its quest for wholeness. She was the only real love and intimacy in his life and that knowledge tortured him because he knew Lara was not real. She was a dream or a vision or a metaphysical experience that he could never comprehend. He could not hold her at this moment when he needed her most and even in the dream, where he could touch her, smell her, hear her voice and share in her laughter, he knew that she would be gone when he returned to waking consciousness and remain as a mere memory in the dusty archives of his mind. But as a man dying of thirst will not reject a small glass of water when a larger one is desired, he would continue to live for the brief, ethereal experience of love and life during the unconscious hours of his sleep.

He soaked in a hot bath and listened to *Debussy's La mer* and *Chopin's nocturnes*; the nightly rituals he had perfected to induce sleep. And now in near silence and darkness he lay motionless and waited. The rain had started again and the faint watery tapping on the window pane was hypnotic and rhythmic enough to instigate the slow descent into full sleep. The tapping rain became deeper and more echoey until it seemed to match the rhythm of his heartbeat and together they marched softly in parallel out of his cold, loveless waking world and into the velvet embrace of the dream.

Chapter Four

Lara was lying next to him with her head resting on his chest. She was starting to wake as fledgling rays of sunlight entered the bedroom. Simon squeezed her tightly as he felt her first gentle movements of the day, but did not speak, preferring to preserve the silence of the moment for a few more seconds. He stared at the ceiling, entranced by the display of rainbow colours that danced erratically. He had never noticed it before and so looked around the room trying to find its source. And then he looked at Lara's hand draped over his shoulder, her diamond ring refracting the early rays of Californian sunlight onto the ceiling. "Did you know you're making a rainbow?" said Simon, his voice just above a whisper. Lara opened her eyes, tilting her head to look at him. The sunlight lit up her face and together they illuminated the bedroom in the warm golden light that always characterised the dream.

"Good morning," she said through a soft, sleepy smile, "what do you mean, making a rainbow?" He motioned his eyes to the ceiling and she looked up, immediately recognising the colours reflecting from her ring. She tilted her hand so the diamond reflected onto Simon's chest, the rainbow light focussing on the silver anchor around his neck. Simon still spoke in a whisper, "If I ever lose sight of you, I'll just need to look for the rainbow and know you are there."

"How could you ever lose sight of me?"

"Oh, I don't know; a west coast early morning mist, a dark moonless night; a change of heart?"

"Whose change of heart?"

"Not mine." said Simon quickly.

"It certainly would never be my heart that ever changes." Lara was emphatic in her tone. She raised her head up and looked out of the windows that stretched the full width and height of the bedroom. They were filled with the pale blue of an unblemished sky and the deeper blue of a smooth, lazy ocean. "Why do you talk of losing sight of me?" she said as she looked back to him.

"Just one of those rogue, uninvited thoughts that drift through the mind; It's when you just know everything is the way it's meant to be and you never want it to change."

She looked to her ring for a moment, "When you put this ring on my finger, you set something in stone, something that will never change. Even if *you* do, I will always feel the same way I do now."

Simon hugged her and in that instant knew he was experiencing everything he had ever desired in life. He wanted to freeze time and preserve the moment so it was beyond the influence of the caprice of life or divine manipulation or the fickle whim of the human mind, but this was a wish too far and he settled for the bliss that showered them both in the golden light of their beach house bedroom that looked over the Pacific on this perfect day.

They had breakfast on the terrace and read for a while in the sun, but then it climbed higher and became too hot to sit in without some shade to temper its sting. Simon let his newspaper fall to the wooden decking, then stood up and stared out to the horizon where the contrasting blues of sky and ocean met and blended into one. "I can't stand it any longer," he said.

"What's wrong?" said Lara, the alarm clear in her voice.

"I can't hold on to this secret any longer." Lara put down her book and looked at him questioningly. "Secret? What secret?"

"I wasn't going to tell you until closer to the time, but I can't keep it a secret any longer. I have to tell you now. In fact I'm not going to tell you, I'm going to show you. Come on, we'll take the jeep."

Minutes later they were in the jeep and pulling out onto the main highway. "Simon, where are we going so suddenly?"

He looked across to her in the passenger seat and smiled as her hair streamed across her face in the warm buffeting wind. She fought to gather it up and tie it in a haphazard ponytail. "It's a surprise," he said. "We're nearly there."

"Where?"

"It wouldn't be a surprise if I told you."

After two miles they pulled off the highway and onto a narrow sandy track that led to a section of sheltered beach. "This is your studio," Lara said, "you're taking me to work?"

"Well, I'm taking you to have a look at what I've been working on."

He stopped the jeep in front of the Scandinavian wood and glass constructed studio. It extended over three floors with the ocean facing side made up almost entirely of glass, allowing for maximum visibility and light. He took her directly to the third floor, where his main studio was situated. As they entered the large open plan floor area it left them with a sense of floating above the ground, as if suspended effortlessly without support or structure. Three quarters of the entire roof was glass, allowing the sky to form a natural ceiling of cobalts and indigos or crimsons and rusts or whatever combination the weather cared to craft. And most breathtaking of all was the glass wall allowing an unrestricted view to the colossal vista of ocean. Lara gazed around the room. "I always feel like I'm entering a futuristic city when I'm here. It's so surreal."

"It never felt right in my old downtown studio. There was something incongruous about designing sea going vessels surrounded by the towers of concrete that made up the skyscrapers of the city. I was designing too mechanically; it was never from the heart, never with a sense of the environment in which these yachts would spend their working lives. But here it's so different. I can stand in this very spot at my desk and look into the blue and it all starts to happen without me even trying. And that, darling, is why the playboys and sheiks and movie stars and rock legends pay me the big money; they know they're getting a quality yacht, built with emotion." He betrayed a knowing smile with a self effacing glint in his eye. "But the reason I brought you here," he said as he grabbed her around the waist, "was to show you something." He took her hand and led her to a large drawing desk facing the window. The desk was covered with a large sheet of black paper that he removed ceremoniously revealing a hand drawn plan of a yacht in blue and red ink. "What do you think?" he said cautiously.

Lara scanned the drawing, a smile coming to her lips. "It's spectacular. Who's the lucky owner?"

He pointed to the name scribbled on the bow that read *Spirit of Lara*. "We are," he said nonchalantly.

"Oh Simon, you're not serious. Tell me the truth, it's our yacht?"

"It's our honeymoon yacht. This will be our chariot and guide, our floating temple that will be our passage to the Orient. I've worked it all out, but tell me what you think." He grabbed her hand again and took her to the free standing globe behind his desk. He spun it slowly, stopping it when the American west coast came into view. "This is us," he said as he pointed to the bay on the edge of the coastline. "I've calculated that we'll need about eight months to do it properly. First we head west for Hawaii, explore the volcanoes, learn how to hula dance and look at Venus from the big observatory there. Then we head south to Fiji, scuba dive with the fish and graze with the sharks and sleep on the beach on the first night of the full moon. Then a little way north to the east of Papua New Guinea and the Philippines and a big sweeping turn south into the South China Sea and onto Malaysia, where we can do some jungle trekking; maybe discover a new breed of butterfly and name it in our honour before searching out the quietest beach on the whole peninsula to stretch out for a few days and catch our breath. And then, it's time for me to buy you your wedding present, which is perfect timing because we're just a short sail from the best shopping in the world; Singapore. There's a wonderful hotel there that we have to stay in, we'll have a suite on the fifty ninth floor overlooking the Singapore River. And when we've exhausted the city, we head east to Indonesia, to some very special islands that are so small they're barely visible on the map. The only transport on the islands is by horse or bicycle, so the air is sweet and the silence is absolute except for the sound of the sea and wind rustling the palm fronds, and there, we will eat by the light of the stars with the warm evening breeze at our back. But then we have a quandary. Do we divert south to Australia a for a celebratory drink in Sydney harbour or wind our way through the Indonesian islands and head across the Pacific back home? I can't make my mind up. So what do you think?"

Lara ran her finger over the route on the globe and started to laugh. "It's just out of this world. I've never been to these places. I've only ever dreamt about going to those countries. It's completely perfect, and Australia isn't going anywhere, so I guess we could decide about it later. But what about the yacht? How long will it take to build?"

"It's almost finished, another two months at the most and she's ready to sail. I had the plans for the yacht three years ago. It was always going to be a showcase vessel to show prospective clients the state of the art in ocean going yacht design and build. But then you came along and suddenly it had your name on it; in fact quite literally as it will be registered with your name." They walked back to the drawing and Simon leant over it thoughtfully. "The thing is, have I missed anything? Is there anything it needs to give it our personal seal?"

Lara looked over the drawing. "I don't think so, it looks just perfect. Why did you draw it in red and blue ink?"

"The blue ink is for the initial outline and details. Then the red ink is used for things I intend to add or correct in some way."

A smile developed on Lara's lips. "What have you thought about?" asked Simon.

"Well it's just one little thing that would make it complete."

"Okay, what is it?"

"No, you'll think it's silly and girlie."

"No, you have to tell me now you've mentioned it otherwise I'll always think it's incomplete."

Lara lowered her eyes and tried to subdue the sheepish smile. "Well, I just thought it needs a love swing right up at the front, where the pointy bit is, you know, those swing seats for two with a little sun shade on top. Then while we're doing the long bit across the Pacific we can stare into the Orient as we get closer?"

"How could I have missed that out from the original drawings? I must be losing my touch. We definitely need a love swing built into the pointy bit at the front."

"Stop making fun of my boat knowledge," she laughed.

"No, I'm serious, we need a love swing. But as it's your idea, you have to add it to the drawing. This will be your contribution to the design."

"But I can't draw." said Lara.

"You don't need to; just sketch in your idea and the guys will interpret it. Grab one of the pens and draw it as you see it in your mind." She picked up a pen from the pot and started to draw, but the pen was dry. "There's a bottle of red ink behind the pen pot." said Simon. She unscrewed the top from the red ink bottle and filled the pen, then drew something resembling a park bench under an umbrella.

"Oh Simon, I told you I couldn't draw. I've ruined the drawing."

"No, it's fine; they'll know what you mean. It will be a fully collapsible seat that can be stowed away for rough weather and brought out and fitted when the sun shines. So that's it, we've thought of everything."

Lara replaced the pen in the pot and picked up the red ink bottle to replace the cap, but as she did so, it slipped through her fingers and fell onto the work desk. Simon threw his hand across the drawing to protect it, spreading the ink onto his shirt sleeve and his hand.

"Oh no, I've ruined it, the drawing's ruined," screamed Lara.

Simon laughed. "Don't worry, it's only the corner of the paper, the drawing is untouched."

"But your shirt," said Lara, "I've covered the sleeve in ink."

She picked up a paper towel from the roll on the desk and attempted to wipe the red ink from his hand, but he suddenly stopped her. "Look," he said.

"What is it?"

"Don't you see it?"

Lara had a quizzical look on her face. "See what?"

Simon turned his hand sideways so she could see the ink stain from another angle. "Now do you see it?"

"Oh yes." said Lara as she started to laugh. "It looks like Australia."

"You're such an artistic enigma. You can't draw a love swing with a pen, but you produce a near perfect map of Australia on my hand just by throwing a bottle of red ink at me."

"Maybe it's an omen." said Lara, "an omen that we should finish our voyage in Australia."

He admired the impromptu artwork on his hand. "Yes, it's definitely a sign. It says stop off at Sydney harbour on the way back. So now our itinerary is complete. There's nothing like a logical, scientific approach to charting a course."

Simon led her away from the desk and across to the window. "It's a nautical tradition that the planning stage of a voyage should be celebrated in some way."

"Really?" replied Lara.

"No, I don't think so, but it should be. Let's swim out to the rock."

"You mean our special rock, our own little nation."

"Yes, let's swim there in our clothes and drink expensive champagne from cheap paper cups and to hell with propriety."

"For a respected boat designer, you're such a maverick Simon. Is it dangerous for me to marry you? Or maybe that's why I'm marrying you; I'm attracted to the devilish rogue that lurks beneath the surface of all that respectability."

He went to the fridge and pulled out a bottle of Krug champagne. "There are some paper cups in the cupboard over there," Simon gestured.

They stood at edge of the surf, Simon with a string bag containing the Krug and the paper cups tied around his waist. A short way out to sea lay the rock. It was almost jet black and glistened like onyx with ribbons of slate blues and greys running through its glassy surface. It was just big enough for two people to lie on in the peace and privacy of the other rocks that surrounded it, shielding its presence from the rest of the world. It had become *their* rock ever since their first swim there when they realised something was happening between them that would alter the course of their lives.

"Last one to the rock pays for dinner," said Lara, already leaping into the surf.

"But I'm carrying the champagne, you need to give me a ten stroke head start," Simon shouted back, but she was already lost amidst the breaking waves as she pounded the water with rapid, deep strokes. Simon lagged behind with the weight of the bottle, but every so often he caught a glimpse of Lara's mane of dark hair contrasting strikingly against the bleached white foam of the waves that broke around her. They swam without stopping until the sounds of the beach lay far behind them and they entered the domain of the rock, where the only noise came from the clash of cool water upon warm stone. They climbed onto the rock and lay flat, arms outstretched and breathing deep, heavy breaths after the cold swim. The heat of the sun tingled against the cold cotton and linen that hugged their skin, but it was a pleasant sensation and they remained perfectly still as the salty moisture dripped away from their clothes.

Their breathing slowed and their minds drifted and as their bodies warmed in the sun, the pulse of the gentle waves lulled them deeper and deeper into a semi conscious state. They were on *their* rock and the world outside was a lifetime away, beyond their thoughts, beyond their needs, for all they desired existed here on a black onyx rock protected by an ocean sentinel.

"Are you asleep?" whispered Lara as she started to stir from her sleepy state.

"A little."

"You can't be a little asleep silly," giggled Lara.

"Well my mind's awake, but my body is still asleep. I'm so unbelievably comfortable; I feel like I never need to move from this spot."

"Hmmm, that's how I feel too. We have the most beautiful home anyone could ever wish for and all I need is our little rock." She was silent for a moment, then whispered again, "Simon."

"Yes."

"I'm so happy at this moment. Do you ever feel it might not be real?"

Simon opened his eyes and leaned up on his elbow so he could look at her, "How do you mean?"

"Well, life is so blissful and I sometimes think is this really happening to us. Of all the people in the world, some are caught up in wars and some have no home and no food and some are just so depressed with their life that they jump under a train. Are we just lucky that we've found everything we want in life? What's so special about us that we should be so blessed? Or maybe we're not. Maybe it's all an illusion. How do we really know if this is all real?"

Simon sat up and ran his hand gently over her shoulder. "You're nearly dry," he said. He looked searchingly into her eyes and they glistened in the same hues of the ocean that engulfed them. "I remember the last time we were on the rock you became all philosophical that time too. Maybe it's something about the rock."

"Well it's so far removed from everything and just makes you want to think. I mean how do we know for sure that this is real? How do we know we're not caught up in some kind of illusion?"

"How can anyone ever know for certain what is real and what is illusion? What do we have but our five senses to assess our experience and make our own judgement as to whether or not we are experiencing reality?" He turned and knelt in front of her. "So what do our five senses tell us about this moment? What does the sense of touch tell us?" He picked up a small round pebble that lay in a crevice in the rock. It was hard and smooth and cool to the touch. He tapped it against the rock and its echo ricocheted between the other rocks that surrounded them.

"That feels quite real to me. Do you want to have a go?" He placed the pebble in her hand and contrasted the cool smoothness of the pebble with the warm smoothness of her skin. She tapped the pebble on the rock and smiled as the echo sang a staccato chorus.

"That was a sense of hearing experiment also," he said as the echo faded away. "Shall we do a different hearing experiment to make sure?" He took the pebble from her hand and tapped it against the champagne bottle. It pinged delicately with the high octave pitch of a child's toy piano. Its sound was sweet and gentle and resonated just long enough until the next gust of sea breeze swept it away with its own inimitable voice. "Let's try the sense of smell," said Simon. "Breathe in deep. What do you smell?"

Lara closed her eyes and took in a deep breath. "Salty air laced with ozone," she said, keeping her eyes closed.

"And lavender," added Simon quickly. Lara opened her eyes as Simon nestled close to her neck breathing in the sleepy aroma of lavender buds from her hair.

"And coconut," said Lara as she picked up the scent of the sun cream from Simon's face.

"So we're convinced about touch, hearing and smell then?" he said looking up into the sky. "What about sight? Is that French ultramarine or royal blue with a touch of violet tingeing the edges of the clouds?"

Lara looked up, "No, it's more of a cobalt blue with splashes of Prussian blue on the edge of the clouds and the French ultramarine you see is in the ocean, close to the horizon. However I could be completely wrong, I was never any good with the names of colours," she smiled.

"Okay, we agree it's blue," answered Simon," so our sense of sight seems real enough, even though we can't find the right colour."

Lara counted down on her fingers, "touch, hearing, smell, sight; what does that leave?"

"Taste," answered Simon instantly. He drew close to her, peeling away the linen shirt from her shoulder and kissed her neck. "Hmm, salty and slightly sweet at the same time. Let's see if the other side tastes the same." He brushed his lips and tongue over the other side of her neck. "Yes, identical. You taste completely symmetrical." He popped the cork on the champagne and poured it into the paper cups. "Let's see how your taste compares to Krug." They sipped the drink and let it linger in their mouths and then sipped some more. "I'm not sure," said Simon, "I think the champagne doesn't go well with the paper cup. It needs a more luxurious vessel to drink from." Lara's shirt was still drawn back over her shoulder. He picked up the bottle and poured a little champagne into the soft dip formed by her collar bone making a little champagne lake. She laughed as the bubbles overflowed and trickled over her breast. "Keep still. This is expensive," he said. Then holding her by the shoulders to stop her shaking, he tasted the champagne against her skin.

"Well? What do you think?" Lara asked.

"I will never drink champagne from a paper cup again. And when we get home I'm throwing away all the champagne glasses."

"It's very flattering darling, but don't you think it will start to get embarrassing at dinner parties."

"No, because I'm an impulsive innovative designer who makes people's nautical dreams come true and like all the best artists, people expect me to be eccentric and not conform to accepted standards of behaviour. So when guests visit us, they'll expect to see me drinking champagne from the various contours of my fiancé's anatomy, otherwise they'll think I'm losing my creative edge." He filled the paper cups again and they toasted the five senses. "Do you still wonder that this might not be real?" he asked.

"How could I argue with such scientific methods? Nothing has ever felt so real as sitting here on our rock now."

Simon suddenly sat up, "hold on a moment, we've missed one. We didn't do touch."

"Yes, we did. That's the first one we did, with the pebble."

"But that was too obvious. I felt the pebble, but it should have been something more subtle, something more sensitive, something so fine that only a heightened sense of awareness in the conscious mind could detect it." He moved closer to her until he could feel the warmth of her breath. "Lips have lots of nerve endings and are capable of sensing the lightest touch." He drew towards her until his lips brushed hers, but so lightly that it could have been the touch of the early morning breeze. "Did you feel that?" he asked her in a hushed voice barely louder than silence."

"I think so," she replied in an equally soft tone, "but I'm not really sure; it could have been my dreamy imagination. Maybe you should try again, I'd hate to have any doubts about reality." He moved closer and touched her lips with his and this time he felt her warmth and he lingered, lost in motionless touch. "Did you feel it that time," he whispered?

Lara's eyes were closed as she whispered back. "Yes, it was the most real thing I have ever experienced in my life."

"I wonder if there is a name for it; what do you call lips that touch each other which such intimacy that it stops time."

"I think they call it a kiss," she whispered.

"Yes, I think that's right. A kiss. We should make sure it's not an illusion and see what happens if we touch lips for longer." So they stayed in each other's arms with their lips touching and the sun was kind and slept behind a wispy cloud; a cloud just thick enough to soften the sting of its heat, but thin enough to dress them in its warming light. And for them, time stood still, though the day grew old and the shadows grew long. Oblivious to the setting sun, they dozed and laughed and made love and drank the last of the Krug straight from the bottle like bohemian lovers watching the world from their island rock on the edge of civilisation.

The sky had changed its palette to the warm golden tints that painted the heavens in the late hours of summer days. "Are you getting cold?" Simon asked.

"A little," said Lara, "but it's so beautiful here and I don't want the day to end."

"Yes, me too, but I suppose we should swim back before we get too chilled; although the day doesn't have to end. We could go back to the house and make a beach fire. What do you think?"

"Oh yes, yes, can we? And toast marshmallows and dip them in caramel and drink vin chaud until the moon lights up the beach."

"Okay, it's a deal, let's go." He put the empty Krug bottle and paper cups back into the string bag and tied it around his waist.

"Oh Simon look." Lara pointed into the ocean. The sinking sun had carved its reflection as a jagged, golden streak of light through the darkening water. "Let's try to swim home in it; it'll be like Dorothy following the yellow brick road. Ready?" She dived into the water, then turned and faced him waiting for him to follow. Simon walked to the edge of the rock and bent his knees before diving, but something did not feel right. He straightened up again and paused. Lara looked on and sensed his concern. He prepared to dive again and felt a numbness in his legs. He tried to bend again but his muscles would not respond. His legs began to feel heavy and unstable. He tried to step forward but his lower body had frozen as if he had forgotten how to walk. "Simon what's wrong?" Lara called out, the worry tangible in her voice. She began to drift away from the rock and in the same moment, the light began to fade alarmingly.

"Lara, wait. Wait for me. My legs, I can't move my legs. Don't swim away, it's too dark." She continued to drift away from the rock, drifting helplessly, not trying to swim, but looking back out of the growing darkness with an expression of confusion and foreboding. Simon tried to step forward and fall into the water but there was no communication between his will and his leg muscles and the paralysis swept him into a feverish panic. From a distant point in the deep ocean a foghorn boomed a mournful wail that lingered in the air and tainted it with the suspicion of danger. He lost sight of Lara and his calls to her were swallowed by the deep bass of the foghorn that now pounded his chest and penetrated his mind, preventing any rational thought. Lara was gone, the darkness was total and the foghorn pounded in his eardrums, and then suddenly there was silence.

Chapter Five

He sat bolt upright in bed, his eyes wide open. The foghorn had evolved into the ring of the alarm clock and he stretched his arm out to silence it. For several minutes he sat still, staring at the chink of dawn light breaking through the curtains. His breathing was fast and shallow and adrenalin flowed through his tired body in unrelenting waves. He struggled to understand why his departure from the dream was so often traumatic and accompanied by distress and confusion. Was there a reason or was it just his ardent reluctance to leave the dream and return to his waking self in his cold and lonely bed; in his cold and lonely life.

But this morning there was a different feeling in the air. He always felt elation inspired by the dream experience, closely followed by a sense of depression and loss, but the anticipation of the next night's dream made the loss bearable, and though the dream was a fleeting moment, microscopic minutes against the interminable hours of conscious life, those minutes became the sole purpose for living, like the addict, who knows his addiction is wrong, but the next dose mitigates the wrong and so the cycle continues. But now there had been a shift that was difficult to define. It started with Damien's dismissal that this could not be anything more a simple dream or even worse, his own imagination fuelled by the misery of his days. It seemed a callous and rash appraisal of the most significant experience of his life, but Damien had no malice for him; on the contrary, he always looked out for him and remained a trusted and wise confidant. And that is why it was so difficult to ignore his advice; Damien had no ulterior motives and only had Simon's well being at heart. What if he was right? Damien was in a far better position to judge objectively.

He felt a reluctant mental urge developing to adopt a new attitude, one of acceptance. It felt a little like defeat, but not the total defeat of an annihilated army; strewn, bloodied and decimated on the battlefield, but more of a negotiated surrender where those who survive resign themselves to a degree of loss, but gain the hope of a tolerable and acceptable future; a different future to the one they desired had they been victors, but a future all the same. Was this the moment to accept an alternative future? Could it really be as simple as taking time away from work, away from his home and those within it? And would a different environment create the conditions for a renewal, like a forest fire raging through the outmoded ideas and habitual thought patterns of his mind, purging the deadwood of dead thoughts and laying bare a new and fertile field where new ideas and patterns of thought can take root and grow and prosper into a real and tangible life befitting of a dream; and what of the dream? In this new, consciously created life will the dream silently dissolve back into the aether from where it materialised and leave him free to engage in the matters of living. Will it be easy to bid goodbye to Lara and wealth and position and the sound of the ocean from beyond the bedroom terrace? It was already happening. He could feel it within. Lara was fading and the world she came from became vague and distant, the way dreams do after the hours of daylight arrive and shock us back into our world. She was a dream and his conscious decision to accept that as a fact cut her loose and brought him back to the rational mind and the world of the material plane. Damien's words were beginning to ring true. He needed a fundamental change; a change of scene, a change of career, a change of family. The thought that he was probably an ordinary mortal with no gateway into another realm and not gifted with the blessing of prophetic dreams was a disheartening one, but he felt the first strands of normality returning to him for the first time in weeks. Pragmatism had won the battle for his mind, the sensible choice, always so dull and uninspiring, yet life enriching and rewarding in the fullness of time, like foregoing dessert for the sake of the waistline as middle age looms or bringing to a close the dead relationship that will lead to finding true love in the years to come. And in the same way he made the choice to see the dream as nothing more than a dream, a fantasy of longing cultivated in his mind that would dissolve as he addressed the issues that blighted his life. But it hurt. The thought of never entering the dream again and the life it offered hurt as if these were things he had really lost in his own waking world. Maybe the dream would return, but if it did, he would now see it as the involuntary mental ramblings of sleep, and with time, it would realise it no longer fooled him and would eventually fade away and leave him in peace.

He pulled himself out of bed reluctantly. Rebecca was still asleep, so he crept quietly out of the bedroom, not wishing to talk to her now, especially in the dark mood that hung over him. He walked along the corridor in the semi darkness, each footstep dragging heavily over the carpet. In the bathroom he pulled the light switch and stood in front of the mirror, staring into bloodshot eyes and a frowned expression that seemed etched into the lines that traversed his face, each telling a tale of the burden of his years. His reflection glared back at him questioningly; it was a taunting, almost threatening look, fuelled with provocation and demand for change. The look unnerved him, but it was *his* look, *his* face, *his* demands; why should he be afraid of his own frustration that was now seeking expression in a way that was unfamiliar and challenging to him? He looked deeper; deeper into the soulless eyes and the fears that lay hidden behind them. But he knew the source of the real fear. It was the fear of letting go; the fear of releasing the dream and the euphoric spell that bound him and shielded him from the truth of his grey reality. But he also knew he had little choice but to release the fantasy and face up to the decisions that awaited his attention. This morning he would walk into Tom's office and tell him he would be taking some time out. Three weeks, maybe four weeks, perhaps even longer. Rebecca would understand and if she did not, she would have to get used to the idea and adapt to the new conditions, just as he had to do now. He was facing a turning point born out of weeks of self delusion which now culminated in the disturbing fact that he was a sick man shrouded in denial. But today began his quest for the brutal honesty that would hurt so deeply and yet out of the pain, perhaps the hope of a cure.

The mirror stared back at him; the threatening expression had gone and in its place he looked for determination or resolve or even a spirit of something resembling a sense of purpose, but these traits he so desperately craved were silent and absent from his world. What he saw in the vacant expression that eyed him was the apologetic embrace of surrender. Resignation claimed him and steered him on a new path where fantasy and dreams were forbidden their trickery upon his vulnerable and weary mind.

He opened the bathroom cabinet and reached inside for his toothbrush, grabbing the handle that rested inside a blue glass and in that same moment he froze in terror. The terror fought with disbelief and disbelief led to confusion and out of the confusion came panic and loss of rational control. He staggered backwards, his hand still holding the toothbrush which brought the blue glass crashing to the ground. It smashed into a myriad of tiny fragments that scattered across the floor, but in his panic he heard nothing and felt only the terrifying grip of disbelief. He lurched forward, drunk with fear, his head spinning with sensations of floating and patterns of light pulsating in front of his eyes. He reached for the towel rail to steady himself, leaving a streak of blood on the floor as he stepped blindly through the broken shards of glass in his bare feet. His heart pounded, vibrating against his chest as if trying to break out from its crazed body. The pounding echoed in his ears as blood rushed in heaving waves to his brain, desperate to stave off the black-out that threatened. He clung to the towel rail as a drowning man might as he fought to defy a watery grave that grabbed at his feet. He closed his eyes tightly, desperately trying to shut out the sensations, but they twisted and contorted and plagued his mind and in his inner darkness he felt himself crashing through the layers of logic that formed the foundation of his beliefs; beliefs that were now shattered and lay strewn on the ground with the splinters of blue glass. HIs body convulsed in fear, shaking uncontrollably, every muscle, every nerve, his whole physical being rejecting the evidence of what his eyes could see, for what they saw hurled accusation at his mind and questioned its tenuous link with the things of sanity. And as his mind revolted, his body reacted and provoked an assault that told of the signs of cardiac arrest. He pleaded with his body to defer what it threatened, but he breathed erratically and shook with spasms that jolted his frame. In his physical panic he maintained the presence of mind to ponder how cruel and untimely it would be to die of a heart attack here on the bathroom floor in the light of what had just been revealed. It would be an act of wilful vindictiveness to take his life now with the knowledge that had been presented to him. It was like retiring after a life of labour and toil only to die before collecting the first pension cheque. And then through his mind's craving for survival and through the inertia that held him motionless and the passing minutes that drifted by he felt his breath slow to a more sedate pace and his heart resume a sustainable rhythm. His eyes remained closed and beads of sweat dripped from his forehead onto the floor. But the shock was oozing away and the disbelief, though monumental in its meaning, slowly began to assert itself as an undeniable fact; an incomprehensible fact; an irrational fact, but a fact in the vivid colours of an unassailable truth.

After several minutes he was breathing easily and the terror had transformed itself into something he was unable to name, but something that felt benign and conducive to a passionate life. Finally he had proof, proof that he was not merely having a dream and not deluded or suffering some mental aberration. He had just been given proof of the material existence of what he was experiencing. He had to tell someone, he had to show them what he could now see with his own eyes, and Damien was the only person he could share this with. Now for the first time he was aware of the broken blue glass on the floor and the blood on his feet. He hurriedly cleaned up the mess, showered and left home.

On the train into work he stifled the urge to smile to himself, but within, he felt a deep, penetrating glow. He was radiating light that suffused the darkness of defeat that he had allowed to consume him in the seconds after waking. The sight that met his eyes as he opened the bathroom cabinet was the sign he had yearned for these past weeks. Why it presented itself now he did not know. Perhaps it came after his acceptance of defeat and his decision to conform to the rational accepted explanations of established *good sense*. But the reason why was not important; neither was how it happened important. The only thing of importance was the fact that he had been given incontrovertible proof that Lara was real, that his beach house on the west coast of America was real and his alternative life of love, passion and profound happiness existed as a tangible truth that could not be denied. And Damien would not and could not deny it, just as soon as he was shown the proof within the next hour.

A dark threatening cloud hung over the offices of Finch & Beckett and a gentle rain had started to fall, but the clutch of smokers stood undeterred in the doorway entrance and huddled closer together to form a human umbrella over their cigarettes. Simon approached the building and looked at his watch before entering. It was still early and Damien would not arrive for another ten minutes or so. He felt too anxious to go inside and too excited to start work until he could share what had happened, so he stood upwind of the smokers in the shadow of a tree just dense enough to shield him from the annoying drip of the cold drizzle.

He mentally rehearsed what he was going to say. Yesterday Damien had responded quite cynically, but today it would be different. Today there was physical proof and he realised he did not have to say much at all. He would just show him and Damien would have no choice but to believe him. He looked at his watch again and at the same moment he heard Damien's voice calling out his name. "Simon". Damien rushed towards him speaking enthusiastically, "I hoped I'd see you. I was checking out some ideas last night and I found something."

Simon only half listened to what he was saying, he was too preoccupied with his own words bursting on the tip of his tongue, "Damien, I had to see you before you started work. Something incredible has happened."

"Shall we go inside out of the rain?" motioned Damien.

"No, I don't want anyone to overhear. It's dry under the tree."

Damien looked up into the canopy of the tree and moved in closer to the trunk. "What's happened?" he asked.

"Well, I went to bed thinking about what you said yesterday, you know, about the stress, the overwhelming problems, taking some time away and all that. And I decided to leave work early and go and look on the internet and try to find some other viewpoints. Well, I ended up getting too many viewpoints and although I came up with nothing concrete, I did come round to a new way of thinking. I woke up this morning feeling resigned to something going on mentally that could be resolved with a change of life. I had decided that you were probably right and intended to walk into work today and demand some time off. But then I went into the bathroom, turned on the light, reached into the cabinet to grab my toothbrush and for the first time since waking up, I saw the back of my hand." He held out his hand proudly, like a new bride presenting her new wedding ring. "Look."

Damien looked at Simon's hand, then confusedly back to his face. "What? What am I looking at?"

"Look again," said Simon irritably, "the ink."

"Yes. You've got some red ink on your hand, but what....oh yes, I see, it looks like Australia. Were you very bored yesterday? I doodle on my hand too, but not as elaborately as that."

Simon ignored his flippancy and spoke with a sense of urgency. "Last night in the dream I was showing Lara some technical drawings of the yacht I designed for our honeymoon. There was some red designers ink on the desk. She accidentally knocked the bottle over and spilled it on the back of my hand. The stain it left looked like the shape of Australia. We laughed about it and said it was a kind of good omen for our honeymoon. But this morning I woke up and it was still there." There was a silence as Simon waited expectantly for Damien's flood of realisation and acknowledgment, but the seconds passed and it never came. Simon began again more urgently than before, "Damien. Are you listening?"

"Yes, of course. I can hear you, but I'm not sure what you're trying to say."

"Don't you see what this means? Lara spilled the ink in the dream, but it's still here on my hand. Look, you can see it."

Damien's voice was strained, "Yes, I see it, but what does it prove?"

"It proves that I am not just having a dream. It's a physical event that took place and the evidence of it is here in front of me, in front of both of us. It cannot be just a dream and it's not just in my mind because you are a witness. I don't know what to call it because I am having an experience for which science has no name. It's terrifying, but it's the most wonderful thing that's ever happened to me too."

Damien looked at the ink stain again, "Simon I know I can see the ink, but have you thought about how it may have got there?"

"I just told you, Lara spilled it as we looked at the yacht drawing."

"Yes I know that's what you told me, but I'm just trying to think of something......"

He paused and Simon filled the silence quickly, "Something more feasible, less fantastic, something more down to earth; is that what you're trying to say?"

"Simon, at least let me finish my sentence. I was just trying to think of other possible explanations."

Simon retorted immediately. "But what other explanation could there be? I told you what happened in the dream and you can see the evidence on my hand. Why would I lie to you?"

"It's not a question of lying. Of course I believe you are telling me the truth, but the truth may have come about by some other means. Look at it this way for a moment, a few months ago I watched a film about this guy who had some kind of multiple personality disorder, and before you shoot me down, I'm not suggesting this relates to you, okay? I'm just citing a case for comparison. It was a true story and he had about three different personalities going on. The thing is, when he was personality A, personality B and C had no memory of what he had done. Each personality seemed to exist and act independently of the other two. The result was that he was doing things that he didn't remember because a different personality type was in control at that time. Now just for argument sake, suppose you had a similar thing going on and you got the ink stain somehow yesterday evening. Then this morning you wake up and have no recall of the incident happening, but what you do remember is a dream that perfectly explains the ink."

Simon did not pause to think. "That sounds even crazier than my explanation. Now you're the one delving into fantasy. How can you even suggest such a thing? Anyway, how do you explain the red ink? I don't have any red designers ink at home."

"But we have red ink here at the office."

"No, the mark wasn't on my hand last night after I left the office. It was only there when I woke up this morning. Are you suggesting I returned to the office in the middle of the night, found some red ink, painted Australia on my hand, then went home with no knowledge of what I had done?"

"No, I already said I'm not saying you have some kind of multiple personality disorder, but just hypothetically and to try to make some progress, what if you have some red ink at home that you don't know about, at least not consciously."

Simon paused, staring at the ground momentarily. When he spoke his voice was subdued, the high spirits of a few moments earlier giving way to a languid demoralised tone. "Why don't you just come straight out with it Damien? You believe what I say, but you think I say these things because I'm sick. I have a mental illness. That is the only plausible explanation for what is happening. You have known me most of my life but still you can't credit me with being able to judge my own situation without resorting to a dysfunctional brain as the cause. The least you could do as a friend is lie to me and tell me you believe what is happening to me. Humour me, at least that way I might feel less of a candidate for a straight jacket."

"You know that's not how I....."

Simon did not allow him to finish." Put yourself in my position, try to see things from my perspective. How would you feel if you came to me as the one loyal friend you could trust and were told it's all in your head?"

"Simon, I'm sorry. I know, you're right, it sounds harsh and unforgiveable. To be completely honest with you, I'm out of my depth. You know I look upon you as a brother and I would do anything to help you. That's why I'm desperately trying to find an answer, and it's true, I'm not being as tactful as I should. But I'm only saying this because I care. I can't just try to humour you and palm it off like it doesn't really matter. That's what I wanted to talk to you about his morning. I couldn't stop thinking about it last night and all I could come up with was the fact that we need a professional." He saw Simon about to protest but carried on quickly, "Please hear me out. I did some research and came up with a couple of names. They sound really good and have lots of experience."

"What kind of professionals are you talking about?"

"Psychotherapists," said Damien, "but just keep an open mind, just have an exploratory meeting to see if you're in the right territory. They might be able to shed light on something we're not even aware of; there could be a simple explanation."

Simon looked at his watch. Not to check the time, for time was of little consequence on this grey morning, but it seemed a diplomatic way of bringing the conversation to an end; a plausible gesture signalling closure without causing offence to someone he had no desire to offend. "I'd better go, it's getting late," said Simon.

"Please just consider it," said Damien as he thrust a piece of paper with the names and phone numbers into Simon's hand. Simon slipped the paper into his jacket pocket without looking at it. Damien turned and went into the building leaving Simon standing under the tree.

The rain had now stopped and the sky was clearing. Simon looked at the entrance to the office and it glared back at him with gaping jaws that threatened to swallow whole any vestige of light that may remain in his tortured mind. It held no welcome, no desire, not even the vaguest hint of responsibility. To enter that building now would be to enter a void of despair from which there was no return. He needed time to think, a place of solace, free from distraction and the petty routines that constituted the grey veneer of daily life. He turned instinctively and headed towards the canal. There was a time when he avoided the canal and its surroundings. It symbolised the dark days when the area thrived on heavy industry, when plumes of toxic smoke spewed from noxious chimneys and men with faces blackened by soot and oil marched expressionless into the factories an hour before dawn. It thrived on the oppression of those desperate souls whose short lives, punctuated with the illnesses and diseases of Victorian industry kept the factory wheels turning. There was no light in this place, not physically nor emotionally, just the blackness of soot and oil and the unyielding coldness of concrete and steel and the certain knowledge that generation after generation would be born into the waiting clutches of the industrial machine and processed into the system.

But now things had changed. The industry had gone elsewhere, like a plague that devours living matter until it bleeds the victim dry before moving on; now the workforces of China and India suffered the oppression of *progress* and the same toxic plumes intimidated different towns and different cultures and blackened the faces and rotted the lungs and crushed the spirit of those compelled to be a cog of industrialised progress. Since the industrial parasite moved east, the land around the canal had begun to reclaim its true heritage. The grass now grew over concrete walkways and the trees bore fruit in season and even the ugliness of the canal, that still betrayed signs of its industrial origins, had had its harsh lines softened by the wild flowers and grasses that staked their claim and grew in spite of the chemicals that once poisoned the soil. Now it was possible to see beauty even in the remaining tell-tale signs of that industrial age: the traces of diesel oil that coated the walls of the canal displayed the violets and ambers and turquoise blues of the rainbow as the sunlight struck the oily surface. It was now a place to wander at leisure and reflect in solitude in the harmony of a liberated land, freed from the long dead echoes of the grime and squalor of the past.

Simon walked to the edge of the canal and sat on a mound of dry grass that had been sheltered by the overhanging shade of a willow tree. He looked into the oily water, mesmerised by the spectrum of colours that twisted and undulated over the surface. Damien's words replayed over and over in his mind. How could he be so callous, so ruthless in his analysis? But the more he thought about it the more he realised it was not callousness. Damien was not indifferent to his plight. He probably really did care and wanted to help, it was just that he was on a different wavelength. Damien suffered from the same scepticism and rationalism as the therapists whose names appeared on the piece of paper in his pocket. Their conformity of thought blighted their ability to see and think objectively. Their minds were manacled by the science of the tangible world where free thinking was stifled and the birth of new and revolutionary ideas and possibilities were aborted before life could take hold and flourish.

But Damien's words still repeated in his ears and the possibilities posed from his internet research the previous afternoon flooded his mind with abstract words that fell like unwelcome rain from a cynical monsoon sky: biochemical imbalances, brain anomalies, mental distortions, dementia, multiple personality disorders; was it all just taking place on the stage of his mind? Was he just a sick man pending diagnosis, awaiting a cure, or maybe just adapting to his condition? He craved more than confirmation of a mental anomaly; he craved more than just a dream. He wanted to believe he was experiencing something that no one could explain, but something that was happening regardless of understanding. Why should he not be the subject of a grand experiment of an unseen source; of a higher power? Why must fear and denial always surround those things that could not be explained? Had not great minds of science flirted with concepts that the establishment feared to voice aloud? It was established thinking that impeded the progress of our knowledge of those things beyond our basic senses. The history of our species teems with firsthand accounts of experiences we cannot explain. They write of *out of body* and *near-death* experiences and astral travel to other planes of existence. These are not the ravings of the feeble of mind, but testaments of the learned elite, from Plato in antiquity through to our present day presidents and philosophers and scientists and doctors who have wagered their reputations and documented their experience for the world to judge. Who are we, the common masses and bureaucrats of conventional thought to question their genius and eminence in matters we can barely comprehend.

Do we deny the pyramids of Egypt and the great pillars of Stonehenge in England simply because we cannot explain their origin? And what of the unidentified craft that streak across our skies, whose presence is confirmed by professional observers, by pilots and air traffic controllers and their electronic instruments that are not bound by objectivity or emotion; are all those who witness them prone to mass hysteria; are they deluded or attention seeking or suffering from some other form of objectionable label that maroons them on the fringe of society. And what of the spirit world whose thousands of recorded earthly visitations manifest without discrimination to both learned scholars and fools alike. Do we denounce their existence and discredit and ridicule the observer because they fail to present a live, fully functioning spectre we can interrogate, dissect and probe. And what of those versed in telepathy or gifted with psychic abilities they are not supposed to own, who perform their art to astonished but incredulous eyes without knowing how they do the things they do. Was it not so many generations ago that they were branded as witches and warlocks and burned to death in the village square by the wise and learned men and scientific elite of their day? And what of reincarnation with memories of past lives and of the ancients who foretold the events of our future. And most telling of all; what do we know of that indefinable force that gives life to a human being. We smile at the quaint notion of Mary Shelley's Frankenstein, where the violence of a lightning storm is harnessed as the source of life for the macabre array of body parts that collectively form a man. But we know no more today about the source of life than the fictional Baron Frankenstein would have known in pioneering eighteenth century medicine. We can transplant organs and connect them within their intricate network, but should we try to ignite life into a lifeless body, even though it may be anatomically complete, we are thrust back into the lower chambers of a gothic castle and left to call upon the power of a midnight storm. The greatest minds on the planet do not know what the spark of life is, but do we deny it exists because we do not understand it and cannot replicate it under measurable laboratory test conditions? Logically, does it not follow that what science cannot conclusively disprove, it cannot conclusively deny. He realised the fact that we do not know everything that needs to be known in order to explain the circumstances and events of existence; in truth, we know very little. We laud our achievements and pace of evolution and boast our technical supremacy with our space shuttles and satellites and computerised lives, all digitally synchronised to within nanoseconds of time, but can we offer a blind man his sight, or a child with leukaemia her future or prevent the thousands of deaths that will occur today from starvation. He knew there was more we *could not* do than *could* do, and he knew there was more we *did not* understand than *did* understand and this gave him encouragement. It was the lack of scientific evidence that would otherwise serve to denounce his nightly events and prove them to be nothing more than dreams and creations of his imagination that kept his hopes alive. What did they know? The doctors, the psychologists, the scientists and the cynics; they were blinded by their own prejudice and lived in fear that their precious offspring in the form of the theories and principles they clung to and guarded so jealously would be disproved, discredited and discarded to the graveyard of debunked science in the company of such erstwhile certainties as a flat earth and a universe with our world at its centre. They knew nothing of any real importance; Simon knew he was a threat to them. He was an enigma that challenged the certainty of their professional world. He jousted with their science and corrupted their theories and lay to waste the endeavours of their life's work. They would package and label him and file him under a suitable Latin term and if no suitable term existed they would unburden themselves of the threat of accepting something they could not explain or comprehend and consign him to the unclassified directory of generic mental disturbance.

He would not give them the satisfaction of entrusting his life experience to them, just so they could parade their misappropriated superiority and patronise him in an attempt to dismiss the most exciting thing that had ever happened to him. He needed no one's validation of his material proof of his life with Lara. Damien tried to rationalise and find a simplistic reason for the red ink stain on his hand. He could not see the truth because he did not want to: not maliciously or uncaringly, he just did not possess the mindset to see the evidence objectively. He could not be blamed; it was like telling the first sea going explorers not to worry about falling off the edge of the world. It was quite rational to fear such a thing because any other possibility was outside their field of understanding. With no concept of a round earth their fears were completely justified. And in the same way, this is all Damien had to work with; he was an old world explorer in a world with no maps telling Simon not to go to sea because he will sail right off the edge of the world into the fires of hell or a pit of dragons or whatever the *learned* men of the day decreed there to be at the end of the horizon.

There was a sense of strength growing from within, a new independence that required no approval, no authority. He did not need anyone's explanation of what was happening to him. Maybe he did not even need his own explanation. He never needed to explain the sensation of hunger in order to eat, he just ate and the hunger went away. Whatever was happening, was happening regardless of his wishes or understanding, so he resolved to go with it; to be the flexible bamboo and bend with the wind, rather than the solid oak and crack in two when a gale blows. There was a shift happening, happening in that very moment. It was a mental shift, an ideological shift, a shift in the very concept of what it is to be a human spirit, existing both here on the material plane and in other planes of existence simultaneously. There was a change of priorities, a change of life purpose. What mattered a few short weeks ago was now an irrelevance, a distraction even, a distraction from what really mattered in these few short years that we lease and call our lifetime. Something was going to happen. He did not know what or when but he knew with a certainty, the same certainty that controlled the beating of his heart that life in its present form was untenable.

For a moment he mourned the loss of the person he used to be, but it was a brief moment, so brief that it barely registered in his memory because now, a fire raged within, a fire that was sweeping out of control and hurtling him towards a destiny that was shrouded in the deepest impenetrable mist, but in that mist, whose secrets were yet to be revealed, lay a life that would never be the same again. His journey through the motions of life would continue but he would be watching and listening and waiting for the sign that will reveal how he can break free of the illusion of his present existence and be released to the one true reality; life with Lara in the wooden beach house at the edge of the pacific.

He stood up and brushed the grass from his clothes. The sun was breaking through the clearing cloud and he felt a sense of light pervading his mind and lifting his mood. He walked slowly along the canal towpath, each footstep releasing the fresh green scent from the wet grass into the air. By the time he reached the old iron bridge his shoes and the bottom of his trousers were soaked and he thought of Rebecca admonishing him as he stepped onto the hall carpet. But she was far away, and her caustic words were far away, and what she represented in his life was far away; and everything about her was so exquisitely far away from the brooding thoughts that occupied his mind in this moment.

He stepped from the soft wet grass onto the textured plates of the iron bridge. It was such an austere object of engineering excellence; severe, black, cold and grotesquely utilitarian. It smelled of aged engineer's grease and the bitterness of outdoor metal, and the fresh rain that fell on its surface accentuated its pungency. The crimson orange coating of rust grew year by year, claiming a little more of the black iron with each passing season, and at some time in the future the rust will have no more iron to feed upon and the iron bridge will disintegrate and fall to its death in the oily black waters of the canal. But it was also possible that this would never happen, because they; the powers that be, had placed a preservation order on the iron bridge. It was to be preserved and maintained for posterity; but not for its beauty, not for its aesthetics, for these attributes were absent to the artistic eye whose sensibilities of beauty were jarred by its crude severity. It was to be preserved for what it symbolised; that brief period of world power supported and maintained by industrial might. The bridge was a link that surmounted barriers. It was a means for transporting the masses, for the carriage of the workforce from wherever they were to wherever they needed to be in order to support the industrial beast and assure the continuance of world dominance. Simon wondered if he was being too naive to believe that one or two of the committee in the town hall who took the decision to preserve the iron bridge did so not because of its industrial significance, but to acknowledge the men and women and often the children who lived a wasted, sickly existence as the pawns of industry whose labours fuelled the profits of the ruling elite.

He identified so closely with those burdened masses, not as part of a class war or the struggle of the proletariat against their unelected masters, but on a more fundamental level. It was with people from all backgrounds who found they had lost their way and were trapped and sinking deeper into the mire of a life that seemed aimless and irrelevant to any sense of worthwhile meaning. They lived for the purpose of survival, driven by instinct in the same way as the lower species that crawl upon the ground and breathe from moment to moment for the sole purpose of the continuation of their breathing. He knew nothing of toil in a factory, but all the same, he was a cog of the machine that drained his energy, that sapped his creativity, that expired the hours of his precious days in return for his daily bread; just enough to sustain him and keep him tethered to the beast that fed him, but never enough to give him the ability to break free of its clutches and develop into something greater than he was.

But the bridge served its purpose over the years and as Simon reached the other side of it he knew his saving grace was to find his own bridge, his own link to Lara, to the authentic life that he only experienced during the hours of his unconsciousness. The great engineers and men of vision built this iron hulk and many structures like it to reach their goals at a time when such technology was itself often talked of in terms of dreams, but they found a way; there was always a way if the prize was rich enough. And his prize was not only rich, it was his saviour, an outstretched hand that would save his life, but it tantalised him and hovered alluringly just out of his reach.

He walked back across the bridge towards the Finch & Beckett offices but the building was absent from his sight. He could look at it but did not see it. Today it did not exist. He would not go into work today. He would not even tell his boss that he was not going to be there. If he was fired, so be it. Let them do it. He had a greater purpose to fulfil.

He made his way back to the train station, his senses filled with the image of Lara. He needed to see her, but sleep was many hours away. He wanted to immerse himself in the feelings and symbols of his other life, to experience those things that brought him joy and peace and wellbeing. He took the first train into town and let instinct be his guide. It led him to the art gallery at the far end of town, the end of town that had been forgotten since the chain stores and department stores and junk food concessions had moved in and congregated near the station. The gallery stood alone, an unimposing building of grey stone and wooden latticework with creeping vines that clung tenaciously to its south facing side. It used to be the public library until funding was withdrawn and the internet superseded its role. Local businesses now part funded it as an art gallery in an attempt to plant a small seed of culture into the area in the hope that it might germinate and spread its branches into the crass and shallow, sinuous streets of the town. There were no original works here, just copies and sometimes copies of copies. He wandered purposefully from room to room, his eyes scanning for images to feed his soul. His attention was seized by a painting of a girl with long chestnut coloured hair. It flowed in waves and the crest of the curves picked up the reflection of the sun which the artist had captured with a degree of skill that belied his obscurity. Partially closing his eyes until they were almost shut he could see Lara in his mind's eye. The hair was the same. The eyes too, matched perfectly in hue, but were of a different shape and lacked the warmth of Lara's. He moved on, pausing at any painting depicting a dark haired female with the elegant characteristics that defined her poise. Collectively the images merged in his mind, culminating into a three dimensional form in which the essence of Lara lived and stood by his side.

As he left the gallery he picked up a leaflet in the lobby promoting a boat and yacht exhibition two miles out of town. Again he allowed instinct to seize control and half an hour later he found himself in one of the giant exhibition marquees surrounded by the glossy white facades of the sleek hulled dream boats. He stood still, feeling a little alienated by the incongruity of a below average income accountant amidst the multi million pound makeshift marina. It was not just the fact that any one of these yachts was more expensive than his house, it was that he had no knowledge or great desire of yachts or yachting or for that matter anything to do with boats of any kind. He felt he should have some kind of affinity with something in this marquee otherwise why did it feature so strongly in his alternate life? Maybe it was a deep latent desire that was yet to materialise for him on this plane. He looked at the lines of one of the yachts. It was like an aircraft, sharpened to a razor point. Could he really design one of these? He walked around the exhibition, oblivious to other people and salesmen and just focussed on the shapes and fixtures of the various yachts. He became agitated by the complete absence of any associative feelings with these vessels. The more he studied them the less he seemed to understand. Now he was not even sure what was considered attractive and what would be termed a bad design. It was no different to when he used to shop with Rebecca and she asked for his opinion on a pair of shoes or a dress. They all looked the same and he had no awareness of good or bad. It was starting to get hot in the marquee and he felt flustered and overwhelmed. He made for the exit, picking his way through the discarded glossy leaflets that littered the walkways. And then he stopped in mid step. In front of him was a yacht that seemed to outrank all the others in terms of its size. But it was not the size that stopped him, it was the fixtures. On the forward deck was what could only be described as a love seat; a swing seat for two with a cafe style canopy over the top. It was just the way Lara had designed the love seat on their honeymoon yacht. He started to smile and the smile grew and began to fill him with the sense of fun he experienced as they planned their honeymoon trek. He walked on towards the exit then turned and took in the whole scene in one sweeping glance. Around twenty yachts were lined up as if in a beauty parade. They were all sublime. It did not matter that he did not know how to design one, why should he? He knew no more about yacht design on this plane of life than his other self knew of double entry booking on the other plane of life. That life was totally different. He was a different personality with different skills and preferences. The two were separate and there was no reason why he should expect to have common interests and abilities between them.

He felt reassured once more and took the next train back to town, returning to the far end, away from the new shops and near to the gallery. From there he walked absently on the left side of the street where a weak, diluted sun shed a tentative yellow light on his path. He turned the corner and into a street with a graffiti covered no-entry sign and double yellow lines that had worn and faded with the tyres of cars that ignored them. He found himself in a jeweller's shop where he browsed the diamond rings and looked for a silver pendant in the shape of an anchor, but they only had a dolphin which looked more like a submarine and a football, inset with a photograph of a footballer he did not know. In the sports shop next door he looked at surfboards and surfing clothes with colours that assaulted his vision with splashes of bright pink and neon orange. This was the imagery of the Californian coast that made him feel close to home and warmed the fuzzy thoughts that drifted through his mind. He found a bookshop and immersed himself in coffee table books with oversized glossy pages of black and white photographs. One book was just about lighthouses. Some were still working, some converted to houses and hotels; others had no role. They were empty, derelict and grew out of the sandy beach for no other purpose than to act as a photographer's subject for large coffee table books. Some were photographed with the lighthouse keeper proudly and prominently gracing the diminutive entrance. The keepers were stereotypically craggy, pipe smoking older men in cable knit high neck sweaters and an expression of understated confidence. They did not seem real, but rather an extension of the photographer's creative imagination delivering the story he wanted to tell.

He browsed a section labelled as *metaphysical* and glanced at paragraphs on parallel worlds and reincarnation. He read passages on hypnotism and past life regression and when he wanted to change the mood he went to the fiction section and looked under the disproportionately large romance section and bought a book about two lovers separated by war in Singapore in 1942. It was the book's cover that caught his eye. It was in sepia with the hero gazing into an empty space, looking forlorn and circumspect. The heroin stood over his shoulder, her demeanour more upbeat and confident. She stared through an open window at the raging war outside as the striped shadows of the window blinds folded around her classic, high cheek boned features. He took the book to the cash desk, revelling in doing something that felt as if it was slightly indulgent. He paid for the book with cash, five pounds and seventy five pence and when the girl asked if he would like a bag, he automatically said yes and then quickly said no. He wanted to walk down the street and let the world see that he was reading a book about love and loss and challenges in the face of adversity. He wanted to carry his own personal story proudly in his hand and let people see what he was experiencing so they would know he was not an accountant; for that was just a job, a label that served as a discriminating device to index and grade him. He was a man trapped in a mind and body for which he had no desire, and from which he now plotted his escape.

He walked through the streets passing faces he did not register and hearing sounds he did not listen to. He had read the first chapter of the book leaning against the dusty, wood stained shelves in the book store and had already been transported away to Singapore with Japanese soldiers bayoneting his door and he shielding his terrified lover with his own body and a Browning 9mm semi-automatic pistol. He walked decisively looking for the right cafe to resume the book. He dismissed the franchised cafes with their cloned interiors, uniform coffee and perfunctory smiles. He began to lose hope of finding a small independent cafe, for every street was monopolised by one or other of the big chain coffee houses. They spread like an unsightly rash over vulnerable streets where any empty premises big enough to house six round tables and an American style chest height counter was seized upon, branded and assimilated into the franchisor's philosophy, where for a couple of pounds or its local currency equivalent you can buy a cup of coffee and not know whether you were in London or Lombok or Moscow or Mogadishu.

But eventually at the end of a promising small street was a cafe with an unrecognisable name. It shared that distinction with other small shops in the same row; a tailor with faded fabric in a window coated in an amber coloured film that was peeling in several places; a dry cleaners that cleaned three suits for the price of two on Wednesdays and a sweet shop whose chemically engineered strawberry flavouring essence was wafting into the street promising accelerated tooth decay for the whole family. But it was the cafe that stood out as one that might offer old world hospitality and quality of service with the charm so desperately absent in the modern chain stores. The facade was adorned in dark wood with the windows smoked in a mahogany brown offering a semi-dark interior, just light enough in which to read but dark enough to inspire intimacy where it was desired. He sat at a vacant table in a recessed corner where a sense of privacy immediately enveloped him. He ordered a simple black filter coffee from a man he presumed to be the owner. He looked Italian, was portly, moustachioed and generally possessed an air of contentment with life and its simple pleasures, the way many Mediterranean cafe owners did.

Simon waited for the coffee to arrive before picking up the book. He studied the cover for several minutes during which time the heroine took on the physical attributes of Lara, and he increasingly resembled the forlorn hero as he pondered the ramifications of Japanese invasion. The coffee was authentic and without any trace of uniform multi-national after taste. He sipped at the hot liquid and breathed in the warm chicory vapours through the wisps of steam that twisted and curled in front him. As he devoured the pages of the book, every so often the front door would open, accompanied by the quaint creak of a dry brass hinge. He paused to look up and glance at the new arrival, something he did not find intrusive or distracting; on the contrary it added colour to the experience. Maybe there was even a hint of expectation, should a girl with long chestnut coloured hair come in, purely for the sake of comparison.

At page fifty four he ordered a *cantuccini*, a twice baked biscuit that reminded him of happier days on Italian holidays and by page seventy three he was ready for a second coffee, but this time ordered a latte for its weaker milkiness to cut through the richness of the remaining *cantuccini*, which he dipped in the coffee in the traditional northern Italian way.

He reached the half way point in the book and for the first time that afternoon he glanced at his watch. It was nearly five o'clock. He would need to leave soon so he could arrive home at the usual time but he also wanted to finish the book and knew it was not possible. He contemplated taking it home but he did not want Rebecca to see it. This was personal and not something he wanted her to know about. He scanned the next few pages then went straight to the last five pages of the book. He thought how mortifying it would be for the author if he found out, how he probably spent many dozens of hours in the middle of the night agonising over a phrase, a choice of word or a sequence of events, but here in one sweep, his reader had bypassed over one hundred pages for the sake of expediency. But there were mitigating circumstances and the book had served its purpose, and as the author wrote as a man of passion and one versed in the complexities and agonies of life and love and loss, he would probably understand.

He read the last paragraph of the last page and closed the book with due ceremony. What he lost in the hundred or so pages which went unread, he gained in the pages he did read and felt he had shared the pains and joys of two kindred spirits whose hardships and ecstasies rivalled and perhaps surpassed his own. But theirs was fiction, the fragments of ideas and creative inspirations from one man's mind weaved together into a logical sequence with a start, a middle, an end and a good front cover to paint the scene. But his own story was real. He had lived through the start, perhaps this was the middle but the end was unknown, though undoubtedly it would eventually be written, maybe not by his own hand, but nevertheless, it would be written.

He turned the book over so its cover was uppermost and positioned it next to the coloured ceramic bowl filled with sugar sachets. Maybe the next lost soul who comes in will read it and be saved by it, or maybe they will not need saving but perhaps just read it anyway. He paid his bill and walked out into the early evening air pulling up his jacket collar against the chill that had set in. He timed his departure perfectly and caught the usual train home, arriving at his front door seconds before Rebecca pulled up to the drive in the dark blue Renault. In the back seat was Mandy: thirteen years old, wayward, but slightly more so than most other thirteen year olds. She pulled herself out of the car with sufficient attitude to demonstrate the degree to which she was incensed, leaving her mother to follow behind. Simon had already opened the door and Mandy brushed past him, her eyes fixed on the floor in a poisonous gaze.

"Hello Mandy. Did you have a nice time at your friends place?"

She stopped in her tracks, looked briefly at Simon then resumed her gaze at the floor. After an intake of breath for dramatic effect she unleashed the best indignant voice a thirteen year old could muster, "She had no right to pull me out of my friend's house like that. She made me look stupid and her brother thinks I'm a wimp and my mother's a crack head."

"Mandy, you won't speak about your mother like that. She's only thinking about your safety. Anyway her brother is too old for you and if you force me too, I will go and see him myself."

"You're as bad as her. You're both the same. All you do is nag me. I don't know why you had kids in the first place. Gavin's lucky, at least he's a boarder and doesn't have to live here with the two of you." She stormed upstairs to her room muttering half audible profanities and slammed the door shut. Simon watched despairingly as she stamped up the stairs. Even at the tender age of thirteen he could see she had inherited her mother's pleasing looks, along with her vitriolic tongue and volatile temper.

Rebecca brushed past him, her face stony and agitated. She addressed Simon without looking at him, "It's a bit too late to try and stop her speaking like that now. I told you years ago that she was too quick to answer back, but you said it's good that she learns to express herself. Don't you think she's a bit too good at self expression now?"

"Come on Rebecca, you know that's not what I meant. I just wanted her to grow up confident and well balanced. She has a fiery nature. That's what needs controlling."

Rebecca snapped back, "Then why don't you try controlling her?"

"When I'm here I do what I can. I work all day. At weekends she's always at some or other friend's house. You see her more than I do. You are the dominant influence in her life. It's you she gets the fiery temper from."

"I never had a temper until you came along. I was always carefree and untroubled. All my friends noticed the change. Within two years I was starting to snap at people, that's your contribution to this marriage."

"Then if it's such a trial for you why do you stand for it. Why not just get a divorce, start again without the draining influence we've become for each other." He heard the words leave his lips, but it was as if someone else was talking. He never intended to mention divorce, he did not even recall the sentence forming in his mind, but he knew he had said it and it shocked him. It was such a dramatic thing to say, so startling and sudden. But as shocking as it was, it was so rational. It made perfect sense. Why continue this daily drudgery of hostile assault, sarcasm and defence. Why carry on with something that clearly was never meant to be? Rebecca too looked stunned. It had been several seconds since Simon made his grand statement and she would normally have retaliated instantly, but she seemed caught by surprise, a suggestion of something resembling fear in her countenance. He waited for her response but none came. He spoke again without thinking, seizing the moment while he believed he had the upper hand. "I don't know why I've never said it before. You're obviously unhappy in this marriage. I am too, so why prolong this ridiculous war we engage in every day. People get divorced all the time. We're not so different."

Rebecca did not seem to be listening. She seemed uncertain of herself. "Divorce?" she uttered. "Are you asking for a divorce?"

"It makes sense. We're both unhappy. Why go through life like this?"

"Are you seeing someone?"

He felt a smile forming but stifled it before it could take hold. If only he could tell her, just to see what she made of it. He wanted to blurt it out, to give her the honest truth exactly as it was. He wanted to shout in a great rejoicing admission that yes, he was seeing someone, but she was not local. Her name was Lara and she lived on a different plane of existence. He looked at her determinedly. "No. I'm not seeing anyone."

"You're asking me for a divorce now, at this stage of life," she said, "months before my fortieth birthday, after I've spent the best part of my youthful years bringing up our children. I could have had a career. I would have been well established by now, but I gave all that up because we decided to have a family and I would be the one to stay at home. It's fine for you. You have your profession, though you moan about it every day, but you have a career. What do you expect me to do as a forty year old divorcee? Go back to school, work on a supermarket checkout till?"

"I never forced you to stay at home. I never made the rules...."

Rebecca did not let him finish, "Don't think for one minute you can just walk away from this unscathed. I gave up everything to give you a family. I'm the one who made all the sacrifices. I have no intention of giving you a divorce, but if you pursue it I will claim everything you ever earn. The alimony payments alone will ensure you have barely enough money left to rent a bedsit for yourself with a candle for heat and light. If you really want a divorce, I dare you to do it. I'll show what a real temper is." She stormed into the kitchen slamming the door, competing with her daughter for ferocity.

He dropped into a chair still surprised at his mention of divorce. What was really surprising was that he had never considered it before. It just never seemed a realistic possibility. It was true other people went through divorce at various stages of their lives, but he had two children at school, he had a house paid for by a mortgage he was struggling to maintain and his career was on the wane before it had even taken off. Divorce was not something that presented itself as a practical step. But of course it *was* a way out. It was a chance to start again. At least for a few moments it seemed like an opportunity. But Rebecca was unequivocal in her response to his suggestion of divorce. Even if it was something he wanted to proceed with, he now knew she would never allow it. He could fight her decision, but she could be ugly and ruthless if circumstances called for it and she would drive him into the ground financially. Divorce was not an option for him and that realisation smothered him and backed him further into an ever shrinking corner.

How had it come to this? He had been snared by a life that incarcerated his whole being; his spirit subjugated and driven into the earth, unable to fly free and create the beauty that his soul yearned; his mind tortured and entrenched in fear of reprisal, fear of consequence, fear that *regret* will be the single word emblazoned on his headstone; and his body scourged by the invisible scars of rejection and frozen by the icy winds of indifference. It felt like a trap had been set by perverse forces that performed their devilish deeds for the sole pursuit of reaping misery into the lives of mankind. And he had stumbled into it naively and blindly and now lay at the bottom of a dark pit, helpless and infected by the virulent curse of hopelessness. The pit was cavernous and empty except for his being at its centre; a solitary figure who had almost descended to the deepest level of desperation that a soul can sink to before they craved the peace of oblivion. In his mind he screamed out, it was a scream of anguish, a scream for help but nothing returned but the dark empty echo of solitude and abandonment. His despair would have been complete had it not been for the experience of Lara and all the things of her world. Had she come to torment him, to let him taste the fruit of a forbidden world; one he can never fully be a part of, or was she the catalyst that would thrust him out of his dark pit of a world and into the light of hers? He knew only one thing; he would not survive in his life much longer unless he found a permanent gateway to hers.

He listened to the sounds coming from the kitchen; the sounds of cooking, the metallic clunk of pans and spoons, the staccato rhythm of a chopping knife on the beech wood board and electric gadgets that whirred and buzzed. He was incredulous that within minutes of a heated slanging match on matrimonial divorce and threats of financial ruin she was busily whipping up *chilli con carne* or apple flapjacks or whatever it was she was creating. It was as if she had the ability to disregard anything of substance in life and substitute it with trivia. Their disastrous marriage with the associated catastrophic fallout for the children was a minor detail compared to the monumental necessity of getting dinner out of the way before eight o'clock. He knew that Rebecca could contentedly go through life not noticing the decaying carcass of a marriage they inhabited. She had no need for intimacy, passion or purpose. She saw him as the breadwinner whose role it was to keep a roof over their heads and put food on the table, at least until the children had finished full time education. His life was well insured, he probably had twenty more good years of earning potential within him and when retirement was close enough to taste, the stresses of the previous decades would culminate in the mother of all cardiac arrests and he would sign out from his miserable existence leaving a very healthy pay off for Rebecca who could spend her late years frivolously on the southern Mediterranean with an orange veneered gigolo on her arm.

He erased the image from his mind and switched his thoughts to the night ahead. He wanted to sleep but was too agitated, so he began the normal process of winding down. He ran a bath and soaked in the humidity of a cloud of steam. He played Rachmaninov through his headphones until the pattern of his brainwaves slowed to alpha waves, his pulse dropped to a sedate sixty beats per minute and his breathing took on the rhythm of a lazy low tide lapping at the edge of the beach. He maintained this state as he slipped into bed and curled up against the coolness of the duvet. It was silent except for the distant echoing bark of a dog that was far enough away not to be a disturbance. In fact the echo had a soothing effect, as if the noise came from some distant point in an infinite tunnel. It conjured up surreal mental images, the kind of which often accompanied the transitional journey into sleep. And then the pictures changed to fragmented images that relived the events of his day, but they were jumbled, abstract and confused like pieces of a jigsaw from two different puzzles. The Italian cafe owner stood on the iron bridge, fishing in the canal with a *cassatini* for bait. Japanese soldiers marched towards him, unseen by the café owner. Leading the soldiers was Damien, on his arm, a pretty dark haired girl with classic high boned features. And nothing made any sense, but then the pictures turned hazy and then grey and then watery and finally totally black as he fell into full deep sleep and entered the dream.

Chapter Six

The silent void of deep sleep was brief. It was only seconds before the silence gave way to the gentle sigh of the sweeping Californian waves and the warm breathy wind that chaperoned it. Simon began to stir and was suddenly wide awake, sitting upright, his eyes wide and staring at the open French windows to the terrace. The sun had just emerged from beneath the ocean, revealing a thin slice of deep orange above the surface. The upper sky was still painted an inky blue; the last remnants of the night, but its dark veil began to lift just above the horizon and the golden glow of dawn filled the empty space with a welcoming warmth. He stared into the light, searching the sky, but unsure of what he was seeking. He was breathing rapidly in short laboured gasps. His skin was damp and clammy and his body shook, not in spasms but with a short regular frequency as if shivering from the chill of an icy night.

"Darling, what's wrong?" Lara's voice was warm and comforting. It washed over him soothing his jangling nerves and arresting his rapid heartbeat. He felt her hand on his shoulder and reached for it frantically, clutching it tightly and then drawing her towards him. She spoke again, this time more urgently, "What is it darling, you're shaking. Are you feeling sick?"

He was silent but held onto her tightly, his gaze fixed on the windows as if willing the sun to rise faster and bring this night to an end. Lara threw back the sheet and knelt in front of him cupping his face in her hands so he was looking directly into her eyes. "Talk to me," she said, "tell me what's wrong."

He took her hands in his and closed his eyes, feeling a sense of composure returning slowly. His voice was weak and betrayed an uncharacteristic hint of fear and uncertainty. "It happened again."

"What? What happened?" said Lara, "I don't understand."

"The nightmare." She waited for him to elaborate but he stared again out of the window, silently watching, waiting; waiting for the light to drive out the fears that lurked in the dark. "It was the nightmare, it happened again."

Lara gently drew his face away from the window and towards her. "What nightmare? You've never told me about a nightmare."

He was beginning to shift out of his heavy slumber and return to a wakened state. "It's the same one. It keeps happening. It goes on and on and won't leave me in peace."

"Darling it's just a nightmare. It can't harm you in any way. Do you want to tell me about it? Sometimes talking about it can help."

He nodded and when he spoke, the tremble in his voice had gone. "I'm living in England, in the north, in some hell hole of an industrial town. It's grimy, dark, ugly and crime ridden, it's a kind of urban cultural desert that lies within the shadow of a chemical factory. There are rows of houses that back onto each other in tiny cramped streets garbed in graffiti. It's a soulless place that chokes the spirit and breeds depression and atrophy. I'm an accountant; an unsuccessful accountant with a drab backwater firm on a concrete industrial estate. I hate my job and the firm hates me and I rot doing menial work on a low level income. I'm married to someone I have started to hate, who has mutual feelings for me. The marriage is an ongoing saga of conflict and bitterness. There is no love, no desire, nothing to salvage, just dread and endless fighting. But she won't accept a divorce. She has me imprisoned in a cage, padlocked with financial threats that would leave me destitute. I have two teenage children, a boy and a girl. The girl, Mandy is only thirteen, but she's a rebel with no respect for anyone and contempt for discipline. The boy is at a private school that I can't afford and is currently pending suspension for handling drugs. My life is like an infinite sentence in hell." He stared out of the window as he spoke, but now he paused and looked for Lara's reaction. She looked at him lovingly and squeezed his hand as his eyes met hers.

Her voice was soft and reassuring, "Darling that's terrible. What a horrible nightmare. It's so far from the reality of your life though."

"It scares me."

"If you're frightened that it could be prophetic in some way, then you really have nothing to fear. You have absolutely nothing in common with a life like that."

"No, it's not a fear that it may be a prophecy of some kind. It's more sinister than that. It feels more than just a nightmare infecting my sleep with poisonous images. It has such a strong sense of reality. It affects how I feel during the day. It intrudes into my thoughts at obscure moments, but it's not like pictures from the nightmare flashing through my mind, it's more like memories, real memories of events of my life, things I've experienced, things I'm now living through. Lara, it feels like it's a real part of my life, a part of me. I feel it's going to trap me and entomb me in the nightmare and never set me free. It wants to take you away from me, take my business, my home, my whole personality. It's like a vampire, draining the blood of everything that defines me."

Her eyes watched him tenderly. She yearned to cast out whatever it was that was causing the anxiety that haunted his expression. "Why haven't you told me about this before? You shouldn't be suffering this alone," she said.

"I wanted to say something but I was afraid of what you might think. Even now in the light of day it sounds insane and I feel silly just talking to you about it. But I know it will come back and each time it tries to consume a little more of me until maybe one night I will never wake up from it again.

"Darling that's impossible. It's just a nightmare, it can't harm you physically. How long have you been having it?" she asked.

"I'm not sure, five, maybe six weeks."

"Is it always exactly the same?"

He looked down at the bed, a frown falling over his face, "That's the strange thing about it," he said, "the circumstances are the same, but there are different scenarios, just like real life. It's not so much of a recurring nightmare, but more of a developing one, where the story continues and evolves."

The maturing dawn had brought with it a characteristic chill and Lara pulled the sheet up over them. "Nightmares like this happen for a reason," she said, "normally they are messages telling us about something that needs addressing or maybe something unresolved from the past. We can't ignore it."

"Ignore it?" he exclaimed, "It's starting to dominate my hours of sleep. I just want it to stop and leave me in peace."

"It's not likely it will stop until you've heeded the message it's trying to convey. Don't see it as a bad thing necessarily, it might bring about something good, it's just a case of trying to decipher its meaning."

"I wouldn't know where to start," he said, "there's no reason in the world why I should have nightmares about a dead end life in a rundown corner of England. I've never even been there, I don't understand accountancy and I certainly wouldn't stay in such a desperate marriage. I have absolutely nothing in common with anything in the nightmare, apart from the fact it is me living it."

"It's not something you can do on your own. You need someone to show you the way." She paused for a moment then said, "Let me speak to Sian at the riding stables. She has a wonderful therapist, a Jungian analyst. She's always singing his praises and Sian doesn't serve up praise lightly."

"A what analyst?" he said.

Lara smiled. "A Jungian analyst, you know, named after Carl Jung, the Swiss psychiatrist and psychotherapist. He pioneered lots of ideas on dream analysis, unlocking the messages hidden in dreams, looking for the meaning and applying it to the individual's life. I'll call her after breakfast and get his number."

"You're asking me to see a psychiatrist?"

"A psychotherapist," she responded quickly. "There's nothing wrong with it. Anyone who's anyone in California has a therapist. We need to do something. You can't go on suffering this way. It's probably nothing. You're working so hard on so many things and maybe you just need to take some time out. But the therapist can work on this with you and try to find a cause and put an end to it."

He pulled her closer to him, "Do you think I'm losing my mind?"

"No, I think you're suffering from something that millions of people suffer from every day. It's just overwork and a hyperactive mind. We'll get help. I just don't want you to worry about it anymore." They slipped back down beneath the sheets and as the golden light filling the room adjusted its tint to the lemon yellow of a rising sun Lara drifted into a light sleep while Simon settled back uneasily into his pillow, restless, troubled and watchful.

Simon sipped the last drops of his breakfast coffee under a shady parasol on the rear sun terrace. He twirled his teaspoon hypnotically in a bowl of brown sugar granules, his mind recycling the nightmares and their twisted tales. Lara's voice carried from the kitchen as she talked enthusiastically on the phone. She was just finishing a conversation and then ran out onto the sun terrace excitedly, "Simon, it's all fixed. We're so lucky, he had a free slot available."

Mesmerised in thought he was startled back into the moment spilling the glistening sugar granules onto the table, "Who?"

"The psychotherapist. I just got his number from Sian and called him. He sounds so nice. He's just had a cancellation so he has a free slot this morning and said he will see you, 11.30. We need to get ready."

"This morning? But that's so soon, I thought......."

"You thought you could get out of it. Why put it off? He's really in demand so we should jump at the chance."

"But Lara I haven't thought it through. I don't know what to say or how to say it yet."

"That's what he's there for. You don't have to prepare anything, just turn up and things will unfold. I'm only pushing you because I saw the look on your face this morning and I can't bear the thought of you suffering with this. It's for both of us. Your happiness is my happiness sweetheart." And that last statement was all he needed to convince him that he should get ready and make the 11.30 appointment.

They stayed on the coastal highway for twenty minutes then turned off for the freeway. Lara drove, leaving Simon alone with his thoughts and free of any distraction. She turned off the BMW's climate control and opened all the windows. She always preferred to drive with the windows open; she said it added to the experience of controlling of the car, being buffeted by the crosswinds and feeling the nuances of the fine adjustments necessary for a smooth ride. It was this innocent enthusiasm that Simon loved to watch as she drove. She had a look of *first love* excitement about her, like it was her first drive as a teenager heading for the beach in a white convertible with her hair streaming in the ocean breeze and a basket of fried chicken and a Frisbee on the back seat. But this morning his attention was elsewhere. He stared out of the side window, not seeing, but entranced by the blur of coloured streaks rushing by. He remained pensive for the whole journey and as the car pulled into a parking bay outside the psychotherapist's office he was jolted back into the present. "That was quick," he said, "are we here already?"

"Already? We've been driving for fifty five minutes. You've been far away," smiled Lara.

They sat in a small impersonal waiting room that smelled of furniture polish. Simon fidgeted with a loose button on his jacket and when the button finally came off, he fidgeted with the loose remnant of thread left behind. Lara placed her hand on his and said "You're nervous darling. There's nothing to be worried about."

He looked at her without speaking, forcing a smile in acknowledgement, but the smile spoke more than words for it gave voice to the apprehension concealed in his eyes. When the receptionist called him in, he said to Lara, "Will you wait for me here?"

"No." she answered. "I don't want you to be distracted with me waiting outside. I'm going to do some window shopping and I'll be back in an hour. Now just relax and say what comes to you naturally, okay? It'll all be fine." She squeezed his hand and kissed his lips and turned and walked away.

He looked into the gaping entrance of the consulting room's open doorway and then to the receptionist ushering him to step inside. It had a strange ominous feel. Entering a room was a simple mechanical function he had performed thousands of times, but this time he was entering the unknown. This was the doorway to an experiment and he was the subject, to be probed and analysed, ogled and stripped of the protective layer of concealment to which every being had a right. He approached with tentative steps, the receptionist frozen in her welcome pose, her smile fixed as if painted on and set hard until five o'clock when it would crack and peel away to reveal the truth that lay beneath. He crossed the threshold and entered a room small enough to be intimate, yet big enough not to be claustrophobic. The room was dark, the only light coming from a large oversized window shielded by an opaque cream coloured blind that transformed it into a projection screen onto the outside world where all the elements of life that passed by became shadowy nondescript blurs that faded in and out from across the impromptu stage. Absent from the room were the essential clichés of the psychotherapist's consulting rooms. There was no deep ticking clock resounding from wall to wall, reminding them that their time was limited and any emotions, shocks, traumas or revelations must be played out and concluded within the allotted fifty minutes, just like any good formulaic television soap. But a ticking clock was also invaluable for filling the silences, affording the parties some precious extra moments to think and reflect without rushing in to quell the awkwardness of a silent void. There was also no couch. He thought there should be one, it just seemed more authentic. There was always a couch in the movies. But instead of the couch, there were three chairs; leather bound chesterfields with worn armrests. They bore the creases and wrinkles of time, though maybe it was more than just age, maybe the wrinkles grew deeper with each sorrowful tale of lost hope and squandered life as related by the seated occupants. The chairs were dark green or maybe blue, it was hard to judge the subtle variation of colour in the low light. The biggest of the three was near the *projector screen* window and standing behind this chair was a small framed wiry man who stood to his full height, utilising every last millimetre of his diminutive stature. He gestured with an open palmed hand beckoning Simon to take the seat closest to him. Simon sat down, then the man did the same, taking the large chair by the window. The chair dwarfed him, making him seem smaller than he actually was but he seemed comfortable and content with the surplus of space that surrounded him. His face was kind and friendly with a smile that radiated from his eyes. He seemed the right age to be a psychotherapist thought Simon, although he was not sure what age that ought to be. Perhaps old enough to have experienced life and its turbulence, yet young enough to still feel the desires and fears at the root of the human driving force. His hair was thinning and greying, but these were the only signs of a man in middle years, with the exception of his tailored tweed jacket and striped club tie, both of which could be interpreted as symbols of middle age, but were more likely to be concessions to the office he held and its need to demonstrate the wisdom and experience that only comes with the later years.

Simon looked around the room. It was sparsely decorated, perhaps intentionally so to avoid distraction and deter the outset of small talk and polite references to curios that would eat into the precious fifty minutes of the *psychotherapeutic hour.* The most prominent thing in the room was the display that was arranged on the small glass table to the side of Simon's chair. A pear shaped clear glass jug filled with water and a silver rimmed straight sided tumbler next to it. Behind the jug was a newly opened box of tissues with a price label haphazardly torn away, though the amount of two dollars, ninety nine cents was still visible. Simon mused over the set piece for a moment. It seemed to invite the occupant of the chair to enter into an outpouring of whatever it was that needed outpouring and to engage in a torrent of tears, exorcising the demons within that tortured and tormented, expelling them in a raging flood of emotion. It was hard to imagine that scenario now, sitting in front of a complete stranger, but in the early hours as he awoke from the nightmare, it would have been so easy.

He glanced at the man in the chair briefly who looked back at him with a soft, compassionate expression, similar to a father witnessing a small child tying his shoe lace for the first time. It was a look of caring, one designed to inspire confidence and safety. The man did not speak and Simon looked away; not that he felt uncomfortable, he just did not want to behave in a way that might suggest he was emotionally unbalanced to a man who was professionally trained to identify such conditions and traits. He was unsure how to get the balance right. If he maintained eye contact he might be considered confident and free of guilt with nothing to hide, but where was the dividing line between that and the suggestion of a psychotic stare?

He felt his left ear itch. It might have been a tiny insect, a lose thread, a stray hair or an adverse air current, but he was wary of scratching it in front of this man who was probably analysing him at this very minute, assessing every nuance. To scratch his ear now might signal something to a man trained to notice the quirks of human behaviour and give them names and meaning. He was not going to engage in any gesture, no matter how practical or how rational, that might imply an obsessive tendency.

The two men exchanged passive eye contact for a few more seconds and as Simon scoured his mind for something to say as an opening gambit, the man said, "Is it too dark in here for you? I can switch on the lamp or open the blind if you wish." Simon felt a rush of relief and he smiled instinctively. The man had a soft, easy going voice. He detected no discernible accent, which mildly disappointed and humoured him at the same time. In his romantic notion of the psychotherapeutic encounter he wanted the therapist to speak with a laboured Germanic intonation, transposing the letters *v* and *w* and occasionally substituting an English word to bridge the gaps in his vocabulary. "Most people prefer a softer light in the room, they find it aides easy talking," the man continued. "I'm David Miller. Please call me David."

"Er, no, the light is fine as it is." That must be the cue, thought Simon. He is on first name terms and now he can just come out with it, no introduction, no qualification, no disclaimers. He did not have to hold on to any fear of being judged. He was not going to be ridiculed and told to pull himself together. This was not a confrontation. It was not a battle of wits or a contest of intellects. They sat opposite each other not as adversaries, but as practitioner and client, or maybe healer and afflicted, but whatever the terms of the relationship, they were two men with a common goal. And then without any conscious effort of thought Simon said, "Where are nightmares?" And the moment the words faded from his lips, he cursed himself for asking such a puerile question. It was the question of a five year old, badly phrased and out of context. It did not make any sense. But the opening question or statement or admission or whatever it was that was going to initialise this consultation was always going to be difficult. Maybe the question was not so incongruous. After all, this man was a professional. He was trained to decipher obscure coded questions, to dissect the tangled thought patterns and collate the broken fragments of a shattered psyche, reassembling the parts so that chaos becomes order and wholeness is restored. But was this too early to be cryptic, even though the very reason he was sitting in this chair was cryptic. Time was short. He rephrased the question. "What I mean to say is, where do nightmares exist? Do they exist in the mind of the one experiencing the nightmare or do they exist somewhere else?"

David Miller looked at him, giving nothing away from his expression. There was no confusion, no gesture to suggest the question was irrelevant or not understood. But he did not answer immediately and a corridor of time was left vacant for Simon to fill with an elaboration or retraction or simply to be in silence in the aftermath of his question. Simon studied him. The therapist did not appear to be searching for an answer, there was no hint of him staring vacantly with a racing mind, looking for inspiration for an answer that might impress and validate his role. Instead he seemed to savour this moment of anticipation to the answer, like breathing in the scent and bathing in the rich ruby colour of a prodigious wine. He let the question mellow and lavished in every passing second of the silent pause. He seemed to know how long to wait and when it would be the right time to respond. And then he spoke, without ceremony, without a preliminary intake of breath, the words flowed as if he always knew what they were going to be. "Where else could they exist?"

"I really don't know, I'm hoping that's where you might be able to enlighten me."

"Well where do you *think* they might exist?"

"I wish I was confident enough to answer you intelligently. The truth is, all I know is what I've read and seen in popular fiction. What I *think* merely serves to raise more questions and I'm not even sure that there are answers to the questions. Questions like are there different planes of existence running concurrently. Can we go to these planes? *Do* we go there? How? Do we have any control over going there and coming back? And if we do go, are we really there or is it a trick of the mind; or should I say a trick of an unstable mind?"

"The questions you pose are many and interesting and could be directed equally to a metaphysician who might have a different perspective on them."

"So you don't rule out the metaphysical plane?"

The psychotherapist sat forward in his chair. "I'm just a human with no more experiential knowledge of the metaphysical realm than any other human so I am not qualified to make a judgement and even if I did make a judgement, arrogant though it would be, it would be completely unsubstantiated and as such would be inconclusive for any worthwhile purpose beyond merely serving as a personal opinion."

Simon relaxed back into the chesterfield, crossed his legs and said, "Well, that's honest at least. So now I know where you stand, I should tell you why I'm here." As his story unfolded, he felt the physical reactions in his body begin to take hold. They were the same feelings he experienced a few hours earlier as he sat in bed telling Lara. His heart raced and his breathing became swift and shallow. He felt the sweat on the back of his neck, and the palms of his hands grew damp. He related the events as if drawing from memories physically experienced, rather than the fleeting images of a nightmare. David Miller watched him dispassionately, unlike Lara, whose personal attachment and empathy wore heavy in her expression. Occasionally the therapist would look down and scribble notes onto a spiral bound yellow notepad, but his gaze was averted for no more than ten seconds, perhaps twenty at the most. Sometimes he nodded, but barely perceptibly, as if resisting the urge to acknowledge a statement for fear of distracting the verbal flow of his subject. It was a testament to his professionalism thought Simon, that no matter how outlandish his story may have sounded, there was never a hint of a raised eyebrow, a dubious glance, a note of surprise or any other gesture that might have implied a judgement was being made. As Simon brought his story to a close he felt the anxiety begin to ease and the adrenalin surge reduce to a manageable trickle. The agitation that caused him to shift restlessly in the chesterfield as he talked was also beginning to wane and he relaxed back into the chair, a physical wave of relief washing over him.

David Miller scanned his hand written notes, the worn down Caran d'Ache pencil twirling between his forefinger and thumb. "You say it started about six weeks ago."

"I think so. It's hard to be exact, but around five or six weeks would be close."

"What else happened five or six weeks ago?"

"What else?" queried Simon, but he did not wait for clarification. "Nothing. Nothing out of the ordinary. Just normal things."

"And what do you consider to be normal things?"

"Normal? I suppose normal is..." he paused for a moment, allowing the twirling pencil to fix his gaze as his mind reached out deep into the memories that made up his life. "For me, normal is going through life enjoying a general state of happiness. It's being in love with someone very special. It's my work; work that I love and which I am very successful at. It's my home with the wooden steps covered in sand that lead off the sun terrace. It's my bit of personal beach and my bit of ocean and the sun that accompanies my breakfast. These are the everyday things that make up my normal life."

The therapist again responded instantly with a question, though his tone was relaxed enough to suggest the answer should not be rushed. "How long has this been the normal way of life for you?"

Simon glanced at the passing shapes on the window blind before replying. "As long as I can remember. I seem to be one of those lucky people in life, blessed with good fortune and all the things that I want. Life for me is good and continues to get better. Since Lara came into my life a year ago everything has been perfect."

The therapist turned a page of the yellow notepad and scribbled hurriedly before continuing, "You said the nightmare inspires fear, but what is it exactly that you fear?"

Simon looked down at the floor, the shadow of a frown descending over his eyes as they grew dark, staring into the uncertainty of the meaning of his nightmare. His voice was strained, the words filtered through the tension of a throat gripped by stress. "What do I fear?" he repeated the question absently as if biding for time. "It's difficult to answer simply. There is more than a single fear. The fears are different, depending on how I interpret my experience. One of the fears comes from the fact that my senses tell me I am going through something that is real; as real as this conversation with you in this dark room. What I described to you as my nightmare feels more like a nocturnal journey I make to a living existence that embodies everything I would consider my personal hell. I fear I am being drawn into this place. Each night I have the experience, I relinquish more of my own life as it consumes another piece of me. It is like a parasite, living off my body and mind, devouring me until nothing remains but a vague memory of who I was in the minds of those who knew me. And then I will be trapped; forever incarcerated in a place, the location of which I do not know and at a level of existence I cannot confirm nor even comprehend. And I cannot control it. Whoever or whatever engineers this diabolical game has total power over me and I am nothing more than a puppet, manipulated and played with on a whim."

Simon had been staring down at the carpet as he spoke. It had an intricate pattern made up of swirls that interlocked and weaved and replicated like a giant fractal. The shapes were meaningless abstract ribbons of colour that invited interpretation in the minds of those who felt a desire to do so. For Simon, it was hypnotic, trance-like; it stripped his mind of the triviality of life's daily processes and banished the distractions that fought for his mind's attention.

He looked up from the carpet and back to the therapist who eyed him with the same studious look that all academics adopted when observing a problem and formulating a strategy for a solution. Simon felt it was safe to continue and reverted his gaze back to the hypnotic swirls as he spoke. "But at other times, when my rational, logical mind seizes control, the whole idea sounds fantastic; so far-fetched that it belongs in the world of science fiction. At these times it sounds preposterous that I would even consider such a thing as plausible. And this thought inspires a different fear to take hold. I'm not sure, but this fear seems even more chilling, a worse scenario than the previous one. What if there is no alternative life, no alternative world, nothing more than the machinations of my own mind. And these visions, experiences and feelings of reality are all taking place on the stage of my mind. Does that mean I am on the path to insanity, or worse; maybe I have already travelled the path and I have arrived at my destination. I am here, at insanity. Have I crossed the threshold into the inner world of the distorted mind, a place where my new reality draws it references from a deranged, twisted source? What is this place called? Schizophrenia, delusion, psychosis? Do any of those descriptions fit me?"

He stopped talking but maintained his gaze into the chaotic patterns of the carpet. It felt comforting; detached from the senses that channelled the information confirming how he was feeling. He suddenly wished for a ticking clock, something to drown out the growing silence that divided the psychotherapist and his patient. Why does he not say something, thought Simon? He imagined the therapist peering into his mind, analysing the ravings, the outlandish claims, the skewed logic of a mind teetering on the threshold of reason, walking the tightrope of sanity, or perhaps it was clear that he had already missed his footing and was falling, feeling the rushing wind and the closing darkness of the long descent into that abyss they call mental illness.

David Miller stopped twirling the pencil and held it upright momentarily like a conductor's baton in the prelude to the opening chords of a long anticipated symphony. He then ceremoniously placed the pencil on top of the yellow notepad, pausing to ensure it did not roll off and then laid them both on the round pedestal table beside his chair. The whole process might have been a simple sequence of practical steps with the sole objective of putting down the pencil and notepad, but it seemed like something more; like a gesture; practiced and perfected hundreds of times that served as a silent introduction to what may turn out to be something grand; a revelation, a disclosure, a statement of momentous proportions, but equally it may be something less monumental; a simple observation, a question even, the answer of which may reveal what lies beneath the deeper layers of the mind's mysteries. But as with any study of the mind it could be that there was no known answer and the action of putting down the pencil and notepad may be nothing more than signalling the end of the session. He paused for a moment and then he spoke, "Let us look at your fears as two distinct things. On one hand you feel, what appears to manifest as a nightmare could actually be a real experience in which you are taken to this realm of existence with no conscious will of your own and ultimately you could be trapped there permanently. As I have already explained, my field of study is the mind and this scenario takes us into the field of the metaphysical world. We might both agree that I am not qualified to speak authoritatively on the metaphysical and I could refer you to a metaphysician who could enlighten you on the principles of that branch of study and maybe even espouse a theory that could offer an explanation to the events you are experiencing. You might be content with that, but it will only be a theory. There is no metaphysician or scholar, scientific or otherwise who can provide conclusive proof of the existence of a realm of existence beyond the one we inhabit. That is not to say it does not exist, it's just that we can't do anything about it. So let us consider the other fear, the fear that you are going insane. The very term of insanity; it's such a loaded word, so damning and final and misunderstood. It is often used inappropriately and even abused when it is expedient to do so. But what exactly is insanity? Of course we can clinically define specific conditions, which in the fledgling days of psychiatric study would have been served by the generic term of insanity. Today we can diagnose it, categorise it, label it and depending on the condition, even treat it. Treatment can include cocktails of drugs, hormones and talking as the most common options but sometimes there is no suitable treatment at all, and this is a sad indictment on our progress in the field of mental illness, for in these cases all we have is sedation and incarceration. But that's a simplification and does not help you to understand your own fear of insanity. The term insanity goes way beyond the scope of any single clinical definition. In its broadest terms, it can refer to an instability of the mind. The fact is, we are all touched by the hand of insanity to some degree, sometimes with a gentle caress, sometimes with a full earth shattering blow to the body. The question is to what degree of insanity have each of us individually succumbed? For example, is it called insanity when we look over the edge of a tall building to the street below and wonder just for a second what it would be like to jump; in some cases, even feeling the actual urge to jump over the edge. And is it insanity to avoid walking under a ladder for fear of inviting misfortune into your life as a result? Would you call it insane to watch a formula one motor race and feel a secret thrill at the expectation of a catastrophic crash with flying metal and burning rubber and drivers desperately scrambling to escape with their lives. Consciously most of us are horrified at the thought of such a disaster but what do we call that buzz of excitement at the moment it happens and why do all the television news channels broadcast it in high definition slow motion with a depth of coverage and analysis rarely afforded to the winning ceremony. Is that not insanity in its most ghoulish form? A more direct example of insanity might be when a happily married person with children, a lovely home, holidays, plans and hopes enters into an illicit sexual encounter outside of the marriage. What degree of insanity is required to risk the collapse of a marriage, the destruction of their children's security and ruination of an otherwise fruitful life, all for the sake of the ill judged expression of a primeval desire. But we can witness insanity on an even grander scale than these everyday examples. Would you say Hitler was insane? What about Stalin or Genghis Khan? Few would doubt it, but it always seems easier to judge insanity in an historical context. So what about today? Is it insanity when the duly elected national leaders of powerful nations wage war upon small, far less capable sovereign states under blatantly transparent false pretexts? Is their degree of insanity judged to be any less because they dress in sombre suits and wear concerned expressions and speak of making the world a safer place as part of their rhetoric? But it would be unfair to single out the presidents and prime ministers. Is their degree of insanity any less than the armed forces that carry out their bidding? And then what about the people who voted these leaders into power in the first place and then return them to power a second time to repeat the same insane, destructive actions. If insanity is ultimately a destructive force, devoid of responsibility and dissociated from consciousness then we are overwhelmed with examples of its presence in the world's population today. We witness it when an oil company drills one of the few remaining virgin areas of the planet; when a logging corporation decimates another mile of rainforest; when a nuclear power plant is commissioned without regard for how to deal the waste product or an accident; and when a banker's incompetence or criminality is met with impunity and his ill deeds absolved and losses covered by unwilling and disenfranchised tax payers. They all dwell under the general banner of insanity. We may describe such actions as greed and exploitation with callous disregard for the legacy endowed to future generations but they are all morally reprehensible and transgress the highest of human values, and as such, would constitute insanity in the judgement of most rational minds. Based on that premise it would seem that most of the world's population is insane to some degree, it's just a matter of by how much. So how does all this relate to you based on your two different fears? If we adopt the insanity model, do we say you are delusional, suffering from a multiple personality disorder of some kind, perhaps paranoid? Nothing you have told me is suggestive of any serious disorder of the mind. But we could attempt to delve deeper, maybe try to categorise you and prescribe a course of treatment if necessary, but regardless of whether or not you are diagnosed with something, nothing in your daily life would change. Life would carry on pretty much as it is now. If on the other hand we adopt the metaphysical theory and accept that you visit this place of your nightmare each night and one night you might not return, neither I nor a metaphysician can help you, beyond theorising what you are experiencing. You can't go to the police and say you might be abducted and you can't sue anyone, so once again your daily life will not change, except for the fact that you live in fear of the visits and the chance that one night you will not come back. You see, whichever scenario you subscribe to will have no affect on your daily life. You are still here in the world, doing the things you do, living your life. The only thing that is different is your own perception of your experience. It all comes down to what you believe to be true. And that can be applied to any event in anyone's life, be it a marriage, a career change or a term in prison. What you believe to be true about the experience will translate into what you feel about it and result in the actions you take. This in turn will create your general mental state, whether it is happy, depressed or somewhere in between. If you truly believe you visit a parallel world, that feeling will dominate your life, regardless of whether or not it is real. If you believe you are afflicted mentally in some way, that too will be the overriding theme of your life, irrespective of any evidence contrary to, or in support of the notion."

David Miller leaned back in his chair adopting a comfortable expression with the merest hint of circumspection in his watchful eyes. He raised his hand to his chin, resting his head in a relaxed posture as he studied the changing emotional landscape of Simon's face. A full minute passed before their eyes met and instinctively, the psychotherapist knew it was safe to continue. "Perhaps you think I am painting a bleak picture of your situation, but I have stated it in these terms because I want to propose a third possibility. Let me say before continuing that I would not normally enter into any form of conclusion after such a short period of time. Therapy can be a long arduous process and there is more to be said from both of us, but your experience is one which encourages me to offer a theory. Let me first ask you a question. Are you now or have you ever been afraid of the dark?"

Simon looked at him, a half smile forming on his lips. "I suppose so. Not now of course, but I suppose when I was a child I must have been afraid. I mean I don't remember any specific incidents of being frightened of the dark, but I used to have a night light in my bedroom just in case. Why? Is it significant?"

"Do you remember anyone telling you to be afraid of the dark?"

"Not especially. It's just the way it was. You know how children are."

"Yes, that's my point," said David Miller. "You could go to China or Argentina or Norway or any country in the world and ask children or adults from a diverse range of backgrounds if they are or were afraid of the dark and invariably they will say yes. Nothing needs to have happened to them in the dark and no one needs to have warned them to be afraid of the dark, but people are wary all the same. The fact is we are all scared of the dark because we are meant to be. It's good to be scared of the dark. Of course today we have mastery over the darkness in our eternally illuminated cities, but back in the earliest times of man, jungles and forests were our home and being afraid of the dark could save our lives. A human being's night vision was far inferior to that of the wild beast that preyed on us, so having a healthy respect for the dark and what might be waiting within it was the foundation for survival. The same can be said of snakes. A child born on the tenth floor of a New York apartment would never come into contact with a snake under normal circumstances, but that child will still possess the same healthy fear of snakes that a child born in an Indian village will have, who may encounter snakes quite naturally in his environment. This common experience or instinct is what is known as the collective unconscious. It can best be described as a kind of genetic pattern that applies to all humans regardless of time, geographical location, language, culture or belief system. This imprint is inherited and dictates some of our most primitive and fundamental behaviours. In a sense we all bear the scars of the suffering inflicted on our ancestors, their fears, traumas and the experiences of their conditions. It is our genetic legacy, we are all hard coded with the events of their lives and these have been inherited through the ages; the unconscious knowledge of experiences we have never personally undergone, but experiences that nevertheless touch us and influence us, irrespective of the barriers of time or distance."

"But what does that have to do with my experience?" asked Simon.

"Well today, in some ways, the concept of the collective unconscious is greatly enhanced, amplified and expanded. We live in a time of instant global communication. All the experiences of mankind are relayed around the world in real time, in vivid colour, in graphic detail, in three dimensional, slow motion playback with analysis, statistics and all at the touch of a button from any location on the planet. The nature of the news media today is such that negative news outsells positive news. We will hear of the gruesome details of a train crash on another continent, but a youth initiative to plant wild flowers at the side of the railway in our local town or village will go unreported. We are bombarded relentlessly with the worst events of each day taken from our planet's seven billion people. So we have a permanent digest of pain and suffering and crime and horror condensed into easy to swallow news chunks and delivered between the advertisements that sell us security and insurance and drugs to combat the fear of the things we are shown in the news chunks. So it doesn't matter where you live or how nice your life is because if you turn on the television or a radio or read a newspaper or browse the internet, you are ensnared in an ongoing culture of fear."

Simon nodded, "Okay, but I still don't see where I come into this?"

David Miller leaned forward in his chair. "Simon, you described a very happy life, one you feel lucky to have, one you wouldn't want to change in any way."

"Yes, it's true, the worst excesses of our troubled world have never touched me. I do consider myself a lucky man."

"And the fear of the dark and snakes. You agree with that notion, yes?"

"Yes, I can see how that makes perfect sense."

David Miller smiled briefly, then continued animatedly. "So you would agree that a healthy fear in these cases would be a good thing, because in the long term it will be of benefit to us."

"Yes."

"Then for arguments sake, what if the benefit of fear goes slightly wrong. Instead of a healthy fear, it becomes more of an obsessional fear. And not just an irrational fear of the dark or snakes, but a fear fuelled by the incessant news media diet of crime, sickness, accidents, corruption and war; a new updated version of the collective unconscious in digital form, where we absorb and are saturated by the suffering of our fellow humans around the world. How long is it before this constant stream of tragedy becomes more than just a fear; how long before it becomes a prophecy, an expectation, even an inevitable certainty. At a deep level you wonder why you should not shoulder your fair share of suffering, the suffering you witness every day in your fellow man on the five continents. What makes you so different? Your good fortune takes on the characteristics of a challenge; it's like you are standing up to God; arrogant, over confident, daring him to bring your castle down and crush your kingdom. And this brings fear; fear of reprisal for your happiness and the arrogance of your indulgence of life's bounty when so many others are suffering. Ultimately you fear man's greatest fear, the fear of annihilation. It's not a question of if, but when; when is it my turn to taste tragedy? The law of averages is always working against us; the longer we live untainted, the shorter our odds become of escaping unscathed. So what do you? The logical action is to try to improve the odds. If you could engineer your own disaster, it might avert a bigger disaster. But of course you wouldn't want to introduce anything bad into your life, although you do need to do something to distract attention from your good fortune. It seems that the finger of fate is pointing firmly at you and you need to suggest that your life is not the idyllic existence that it appears. And this, Simon, is when your unconscious goes to work. Your unconscious is the only thing that can save you. Of course it doesn't want to bring a real disaster into your life, so it goes about creating a false one. It delivers to you a dream; dreams being the voice, the manifestation of the unconscious. This dream, which understandably you describe as a nightmare, delivers the hellish life that your unconscious mind believes will save you from a real world disaster. In the dream you are miserable. You have an unhappy marriage, unruly children, a dead end career that you hate and in which you feel trapped. There is so much misery in your dream life that fate, in all its mercy could never deliver any further burden to you. In a way you are saying to God 'don't pick on me, I have a terrible life already, pick on someone else'. And through this, hopefully the dark side of life or disciples of the grim reaper will not visit you. And this is what your unconscious is banking on; this is its solution to the problem, a problem that doesn't actually exist except as a common, universal human fear in your mind. The unconscious will often act in such a way so as to derive what it believes to be a benefit, and this it thinks it is doing, but sometimes it results in some form of hardship or disquiet in the conscious mind and body. This situation can only be resolved by understanding the communication from the unconscious and acting accordingly. In some parts of India, a small black mark is applied to the forehead of children. This is designed to mar the child's beauty, thereby not attracting the attention of evil spirits. It is possible that your nightmare is the equivalent of this black mark. It mars your life symbolically in the hope of distracting the dark side of fate and averting personal tragedy."

The psychiatrist eased back in his seat again and allowed Simon the space to reflect or object or simply be in silence with whatever emotions embraced him. Simon rubbed his eyes. He felt a wave of tiredness and a sense of confusion that overwhelmed him. He wanted an unequivocal answer, even if the answer condemned him, for that was better than the unknown, undefined fears that the mind used so skilfully and devilishly to orchestrate abominations of its own that were often far more sinister than the true threat. He wanted to be told he was suffering from something that was well known and documented in medical literature and could be treated like any other ailment. Or if it was not a sickness of the mind, then a possession, a visitation, a Machiavellian spirit in an act of devilry that could be thwarted by a specialist versed in the ways of the occult. But he had nothing; nothing more than a theory that a psychotherapist proposed as a possibility; no commitment, no concrete diagnosis and no conclusion to the terrors that plagued him. "So what can I do now David?"

"If what I am suggesting is correct, then we both have work to do, but especially you. Your unconscious is speaking to you in no uncertain terms. In a sense it is overcompensating, even out of control. You must discover and heed its true message. What is the real thing that you fear and how do you go about assuaging that fear and accepting the uncertainties that we all must face in life. This, if you choose to take it on is the work that awaits you. But we can only know if this is the source of your disturbance by tackling it head on and going deeper into the experience."

David Miller glanced at his watch and then back to Simon. His tone was slightly lighter as he spoke. "We've covered a lot here today Simon. Why don't you go and think things over at your own pace. Live with the idea for a few days and see how it feels. If you would like me to work with you I am happy to take you on as a client, but don't rush your decision. Decisions of this type tend to make themselves. It's often more of an instinctive thing than one you intellectualise. Maybe you could give me a call next week and we'll take it from there."

 As they left the office, Simon turned and said, "Thank you for the insight. It's been, well, enlightening. I will think about what you've said and call you in a few days." He smiled at the receptionist and made his way to the double glass doors to exit the building. He could see Lara in the car outside. He pushed the door, but it was locked.

"Oh sorry," said the receptionist as she pressed a button next to her desk. A loud electronic buzz sounded next to the door, "The door's open now," she continued. Simon pushed the door but it would still not open. The receptionist pressed the button again and the buzz sounded, but despite pushing and pulling the door it would not budge. Lara was waving from the car, beckoning him forward. Simon silently mouthed the words through the glass door, 'I'm coming, the door's stuck'.

"It's always sticking," said the receptionist, the embarrassment growing in her voice. She pressed the button repeatedly, like a Morse code operator frantically relaying a message. "Give it a good hard nudge." Simon pushed again, the repeated buzzing sound drowning out the rattle of the door. He looked out at Lara who was looking increasingly bemused. The buzzing became louder and the receptionist's voice took on a strange echoing quality as if she was fading out of the room. As Simon felt the beginnings of panic, the buzzing sound became intolerably loud and repetitive and then a dark curtain fell across his vision for the briefest moment as he slipped abruptly out of the dream.

Chapter Seven

He opened his eyes wide, momentarily startled by the sudden return to wakefulness, then reached out urgently to silence the buzzing alarm clock on the bedside table. His first thought was that it was Saturday and he did not have to go to work. He realised he must have set the alarm clock without thinking the night before. He looked at the chink in the curtains and saw the thin slit of grey announcing another day of dark cloud and rain. He lay back on the pillow and ran the closing stages of the dream through his mind, the way he always did, but something about the dream's content felt different this time and he tried to examine what it was that unsettled him. And then, suddenly it struck him and his stomach lurched with a physical reaction. He remembered he was in a psychotherapist's office, but what shocked and disturbed him was the fact that he had been discussing his real waking life. It seemed preposterous; even by the bizarre laws that ruled his life, this seemed impossible: his dream self was talking to a psychotherapist about his real existence in England, about the wife who hated him, about his lawless children, his detestable job, everything that defined his true existence; the man, the accountant, the dreamer of his dreams. But in talking to the psychotherapist, his dream self described his English life as a nightmare, not as a figure of speech, but as a real nightmare taking place in the mind of his dream self. For the first time it dawned on him that his dream self was aware of his true waking existence. The marine architect from west coast America who lived in a house on the beach was having nightmares that he was an accountant from a grim suburb in the north of England who lived in a semi-detached house on a rundown street. He had become the nightmare of his dream.

His mind raced frantically. What was the implication of this new development? Maybe it was not a new development at all, perhaps he was just never aware of it before. Maybe it had no bearing on anything, but something unnerved him. It was a niggling thought that persisted that this might be the first crack to appear in the idyll of his dream. And then it came to him in the dark foreboding cloud of realisation. His dream self was seeking the help of a psychotherapist, but for what purpose? There could only be one reason within his otherwise perfect life; it was to rid him of his nightmare. He was trying to exorcise the accountant and his dismal life in the same way a demonic presence would be cast out. But this could not be allowed to happen. There was no way of knowing for sure, but this could end the dream forever. He did not know what rules governed his experience but he had to stop any further sessions between his dream self and the psychotherapist. It could destroy everything. But he struggled to understand how could he do this? In the dream, he was a different personality, he had different thoughts. In the dream moment, as far as he was concerned he was only experiencing reality; the beach house, Lara, the engagement ring on her finger; these were the tangible things of his life. How was he going to force his dream self to abandon the idea of seeing the psychotherapist to bring the nightmare to an end? One thing he knew for certain was that if the dream stopped, his life would be meaningless. There would be nothing left to live for and it would signal the end of everything.

He sat alone at breakfast while Rebecca busied herself noisily in the kitchen. His mind contemplated the dilemma that threatened to shatter his strange ethereal world. He tried to apply logic to a situation which was outside the realms of the universal laws that dictated life. He pushed his coffee away in annoyance as Rebecca came out of the kitchen. "The bathroom light has blown," she said, "can you change it please; I'm just going to run a bath." He grunted acknowledgment and dragged the coffee cup back so he could linger at the table a few moments longer. The more he pondered on the problem, the more he felt he was losing rationality. But there was very little that was rational in his life. This new phase had changed everything. He was now thinking in terms of two people, the accountant and the marine architect, each on a different life path with different thoughts and perspectives. They were both Simon and both connected, but seemingly two different entities, independent, in two different places and times. How could one possibly influence the other?

He wandered into the kitchen and picked up a new light bulb from a drawer, then made his way absently upstairs to the bathroom, all the time his mind muddled, his thoughts going round in circles. The bathroom was filling with steam from the running bath water and condensation fogged the mirrors and chrome fittings. "Rebecca. Where's the step ladder? I left it on the landing." he called out.

Rebecca's voice came back faintly from the bedroom. "I put it back in the shed where it belongs."

Simon cursed under his breath, then looked round for something to stand on so he could reach the light fitting in the ceiling. There was nothing suitable within reach, but the light was directly above the bath so he climbed up onto the edge of the bath and from there unscrewed the fused light bulb. It was difficult to see in the steam but he managed to fit the new bulb just as Rebecca entered. "Are you insane?" she yelled, "you haven't turned off the mains power and you're balancing on the edge of the bath above running water in a room full of steam. If you're trying to kill yourself, you're going the right way about it."

And in that split second of time, Simon suddenly knew what he had to do. It was like a revelation, a lightning bolt of intention into the core of his creative mind. Rebecca continued talking but her words were indiscernible, just a wall of background noise that blended with the gurgling symphony of running water. He stood motionless on the edge of the bath, mesmerised by the fog of steam, enraptured by the brilliance of his idea. But he could not take full credit for it. It was Rebecca's inspiration, albeit unintentional, but it was her timely sarcasm that unveiled the plan. He echoed her words in his mind, *if you're trying to kill yourself.* And that was it; brilliant in its simplicity. Why had he not thought of it himself? It made perfect sense. There was only one thing preventing him from staying in the dream and living a perfect life and that was waking up out of sleep. The moment he was clawed back into his grim world, the dream ceased to be. But what if he was dead? What if he died in his sleep during a dream? He would never wake up again. There would be no life to return to. He would have to remain in the dream. He considered the possibility that his bodily death might end the dream too, but he knew his consciousness had transferred to the other realm during sleep. During the sleep phase he unequivocally had no consciousness in his own sleeping body, but his consciousness continued to exist completely independently; it lived and thrived and laughed and lay in the sun and made love in the existence of his beautiful alternative life. So if consciousness were never permitted to return to his body, because there was no waking body to return to, as in the case of death, he would be free to remain where he was. He will have severed the tie to a life he detested, a life that dragged him back from his blissful, perfect world through the process of waking.

He had found the gateway to liberty; suicide: such a dark word, yet filled with the light of beautiful things to come.

He ran downstairs and out into the garden. At the farthest end was the pear tree under which he often sat to think. It was cold and water droplets from the earlier rain fell intermittently from the branches of the tree but Simon was aware of little beyond the plan of action that now fully occupied his mind. The method of suicide was not the difficult part. He could always devise a way. Man, over the centuries had devised more methods of taking a life than preserving one, so he was spoiled for choice. The real problem was timing. His logic told him he had to die while he was actively in the dream but timing this would be vague and uncertain. He would prefer to do it alone, but he needed an accomplice, someone he could trust but would also understand. There was only one person that came to mind. Damien. He was certainly trustworthy, but would he understand? Maybe not, but there was little choice. There was no one else he could consider. They had their usual golf round planned for eleven o'clock and that is when he would ask.

On the way to the golf course Simon mentally rehearsed what he would say. He practised several versions but each one sounded more outrageous than the previous attempt, so he had to stop thinking about it before he lost confidence altogether. The fact was, there was no easy way to ask someone to assist in an act of suicide and nothing was going to make it sound like a rational request.

They played the first five holes with only the minimal exchange of words and it was on the green of the sixth hole that Damien finally stated what was plainly obvious. "Come out with it Simon, I can see your mind is not on this game, you're playing like you've never held a club in your hand before."

"Am I playing that badly? Well, you're always so perceptive Damien. I can't keep anything from you can I?"

"Since we were in the car park I've been wanting to ask how things have been developing with you, but you didn't volunteer anything so I just thought I should let you talk in your own time."

Simon finished his putt then looked warily into the grey sky. "Do you think the rain will hold off until we finish?"

"Come on Simon, stop stalling. Just come out and say it. You're giving me palpitations with the anticipation."

"Okay, okay, let's walk to the next hole as we talk." They collected their golf bags and walked to the seventh hole where Simon continued. "I know it's been difficult for you Damien, listening to me telling you about my experience. It must sound so outlandish, even completely insane. I do understand how you have had trouble wondering how to respond and I know you have gone of your way to try to help me, even though you see things differently to the way I see them. But sometimes in life you just have to go with something and follow it, even though you maybe don't understand it. And that's what I want to ask of you now; to just go with something even though you probably won't be able to understand it. I don't understand it myself, but we don't necessarily have to understand something in order to do it, do we?"

Damien placed his ball on the tee. "Let's not tee off yet, not until you've told me what it is you want. I have a feeling I'm going to end up in the rough on this hole."

"Well in a sense I'm already in the rough and this is my way of getting out of it. I've come to a decision. It's a big decision, but it's not what it may seem to be at first sight, but I do need your help. I've decided to end things here."

"Here? What do you mean, here? The golf?"

"No. I mean end it, end it all."

"I'm not sure what you're ending Simon. Are you talking about the job, your marriage? What?"

"Yes, that's right. All of it. I'm ending the job, the marriage, the golf, the house, the children, everything."

"Hold on a moment Simon, I know we talked about you having a complete break, but this is a really major move. Where are you going to go? Do you have somewhere in mind?"

"Yes. I know exactly where I'm going. I'm going to the life that I visit in my dream, but I won't be coming back again."

"Simon, I thought you were being serious. You know that's not possible. Exactly how do you believe you can do such a thing?"

"Very simply. I told you. By ending it all. I'm going to end my life. Kill myself. Suicide."

Damien dropped his club on the ground. "I wish I could respond by saying something intelligent, but it's difficult to reply intelligently to what sounds like the insane ramblings of a madman. Simon, what's happening to you? We talked about this. I thought things were okay and you were going to take a rest. I know things aren't good, but it doesn't call for suicide. That doesn't resolve anything"

"No, no you don't understand. I'm not just killing myself to escape a hopeless life; I'm doing it to go forward to a meaningful life, one that I already enjoy but only temporarily. This is nothing more than making it permanent. Don't think of it as suicide in the normal sense of the word, of course that would be terrible, but just try to see things from my point of view and you will see the situation in a whole new light."

Damien picked up his club from the ground and threw it carelessly back into the bag. "Simon, I can never see things from your point of view if you persist in talking this way. I can't even have a sensible discussion with you if this is what you truly believe. If I see things from your perspective I am just pandering to the sickness or whatever it is that has gripped you. It would be completely wrong of me. I would just be feeding a delusion of some sort rather than trying to help my best friend, don't you see that?"

"I know that's how it seems to you and honestly, I don't blame you. I think I would feel the same if our roles were reversed. But you don't have the knowledge I have; you haven't experienced what I have experienced, so you can't possibly know. You are in the same position as an ancient civilisation living in the shadow of an erupting volcano who offer sacrifices to it to appease its apparent fury. You couldn't blame them because they had no knowledge or experience of geology to know any better. Can you not just suspend any notions of what is or isn't possible within the forces of life and death and have some faith in what I have shared with you?"

"I can't do that, because you would be asking me to go against what I believe to be right. You would be asking me to contribute to your demise. It's because I care about you and your welfare that I can't just accept what you say. Anyway you said you need my help. In what way?"

"Unless you change your view and share in my beliefs, there's little point in asking you." Damien was staring at the ground and remained silent so Simon continued. "You see I can't do this alone. I need to die while I'm actively in the dream state and this means I need someone to do it: you Damien, my one true friend on earth. It would be quite easy. You see, it's possible to detect when a person is dreaming by their eye movements, it's called REM sleep, rapid eye movement. You just wait until I'm asleep, watch for my eye movements beneath my eyelids and then..."

Damien interrupted sharply, "...and then drive a stake through your heart. Isn't that how it's meant to go? And then behead you before the sun rises. Or is it a silver bullet through the heart? I always seem to get my myths and legends mixed up. Still, we can always look it up in the world encyclopaedia of witchcraft and sorcery; I'd hate to get it wrong when so much depends on it."

"I'm sorry you can't see things my way Damien. Sometimes the greatest gesture of true friendship is blind faith beyond what the eye sees. I hoped I could have counted on your friendship for that."

"But you know very well you can always count on my friendship. I have always acted genuinely towards you. I have and will continue to do all those things that best friends are supposed to do. I will take away your car keys when you've drunk too much and are threatening to drive home. I will cover for you if your wife asks questions about your indiscretions. I will tell you you're not over the hill when you turn fifty. I will do all those things that friends are there to do. But I have to draw the line somewhere and that means I will not murder you. That may sound strange in your present state of mind, but it goes beyond the bounds of friendship."

"It's not murder."

"What do you mean, it's not murder?"

"Well you have my consent. I don't think they can call it murder in a court of law, not when the other party is willing. I think it's called assisted suicide."

Damien threw his hands up in the air. "I can't believe I'm standing in the middle of a golf course having a discussion on a point of law relating to the unlawful killing of my best friend. You're making me as crazy as you are. It doesn't matter what it's called, I would be thrown into prison for life and that would be your legacy to me, which says a lot for your friendship towards me. Anyway, I don't want to discuss this anymore. If you persist in this suicide idea I have a responsibility to do something. I will go to the police or the medical authorities or whoever I need to. I'm sure I can have you sectioned under a mental health act. I don't want to do this but you are forcing me. It's for your health, for your own good. I also have to think of Rebecca and your children, even though they're probably driving you part of the way there, but still, they do not deserve to be without a husband and father."

"Okay Damien, calm down, I didn't mean to upset you. You've made your point. I just wanted to get your reaction and I understand you think it's insane. So shall we finish the game and forget I said anything."

"What? Just forget you plan to kill yourself and continue our round of golf."

"If you had agreed with me, it would have lent some credibility and validity to the way I was feeling, but you don't even see the vaguest glimmer of sense in anything I've said. So where does that leave me? I'm now questioning the sense in the whole idea myself."

Damien nodded his head unconsciously and felt the severity of his expression ease. He drew a club from his bag and lined up with the tee. "Just don't go quiet on me Simon, okay? Because I don't agree with you doesn't mean I don't care about you. We will resolve this current crisis together and it won't involve suicide."

They talked little for the rest of the game except for the complimentary exchanges of fellow golfers in courteous admiration of each other's swing. As they drew towards the last holes, the sky was blending a palette of its deepest greys and by the seventeenth had painted itself in the ominous cold hue of an impending storm. Damien glanced up periodically and could not help but wonder if this was a portent for the coming days of his best friend. But for Simon, it was quite different. The leaden skies symbolised everything he would shortly be leaving behind. But he worried whether his display of compliance to Damien's point of view was convincing enough. He thought that perhaps it was lacking, a little too obliging too suddenly. But what other choice did he have? He had to hope he had done enough to deter Damien from doing anything that might complicate his intentions. It was already going to be difficult. He had no accomplice and no method that could be called foolproof, but the decision had been made and now he could devote his full attention to the practical matter of how he was going to die.

Shortly before completing the eighteenth hole the heavens split open and a deluge of cold, relentless rain brought an abrupt end to the game. They raced back to their cars and as Damien watched Simon driving away he hoped with every fibre of wisdom he possessed that he had said the right thing.

The rain intensified as Simon joined the motorway. To him it seemed as if he was driving through a watery tunnel, the windscreen wipers carving out a narrow tube through which he sped. He felt cosseted from the rest of the world and free to let his mind roam and scheme and find a solution to the problem that held him captive within the sarcophagus of his waking days. Snuffing out his life was easy; the complication was doing it while safe in the arms of his dream. He thought of asking Rebecca. She could do it without any emotional attachment, but she would refuse on financial grounds. He was the breadwinner and she would be cutting off her own revenue stream. He could always entice her with the insurance payout. The policy would still be honoured in the case of a suicide as it was over two years old but if there was any suspicion of her being complicit in the act it could get complicated and she would not want to be exposed to the risk. Anyway, he was not sure if he could trust Rebecca. Out of spite she would probably kill him before he started dreaming and prevent him from reaching his destination. And then he wondered by way of a sudden attack of compassionate thought if he was being too harsh on her. Would she really agree to assist in taking his life? Had his estimation of her really sunk so low? It was sad that he should even have to consider the question. The truth is she would probably not even have the slightest inclination to kill him, at least not in the context in which he was thinking. But, she *was* killing him, perniciously, year after year, in small increments, each jibe, each criticism, each refusal, each reproach; each one a wound that was slowly and unwittingly killing him. And maybe that was a greater crime and more cruel than a single fatal blow. But it meant he was quite certain: his suicide had to be a solitary affair.

The rain continued to beat down heavily on the roof of the car, blanketing any other sound out of his world. The visibility closed in even further, adding to his feeling of isolation within his small bubble in the colossus of the storm. He was caught in that strange unearthly capsule of false security, similar to being in an aircraft when travelling at speeds that would crush the human body on impact, and separated from the outer hostile environment by nothing more than the thin metal skin of the vehicle that hurtled him through space. How easy it would be he thought, to veer the car with the subtlest of pressure off the motorway and directly into the stone and metal upright of one of the bridges. At ninety five miles per hour it would be instant; incontrovertible; final. Could he possibly pass over directly into his dream life in the moment of death? Why should it not be the same process as falling asleep; an instant transference of consciousness away from the mortal body as soon as the brain shuts down? But it was too uncertain he thought. He had no way of being sure if it worked that way. It could be a catastrophic mistake. He had to be asleep first, he had to be actively in the dream. He shunned the thought quickly and reverted to the problem at hand; how to synchronise death with the inception of the dream.

By the time he arrived home, the continuing rain had created impromptu rivers that meandered their way down the slope of the drive, then diverted their route sinuously around the wheels of the car is it came to rest. Simon turned off the engine and sat motionless, entranced by the drumming of the rain on the metal roof. He looked up at the house absently. He felt a glorious finality in the moment. This could be the last time he sat in this car staring up at the house; the last time he would look at the loose gutter on the corner of the roof as it flailed in the torrent of water; the last time he would pause before entering the house, dreading facing the woman that waited within. He felt the rich invigorating rejuvenation that lay in the aftermath of a decision made well. This was the prize when doubt was spurned and sceptics abated to the far, unseen fringes of his mind, so all that remained was the sparkling brilliance of crystal clear thought, sharpened and focussed on the sole object of his desire.

He spent the evening wandering from room to room, his mind absorbed like a military strategist on the eve of the ultimate campaign, and as darkness fell he lay in bed and mused comfortably on the modes of his despatch. He heard the dogs barking in the gardens outside and smiled knowing this would be the last time he would endure it because the next day, Sunday, he would leave this life forever. And as the bark of the dogs faded into a distant echo and the veil of darkness drew him into sleep, he entered the dream.

Chapter Eight

"Simon, Simon. It's okay, you're fine, wake up." Lara held his shoulders and gently shook him out of his distressed sleep. They were on the beach, cooling under the shade of a parasol against the sun. Simon sat up abruptly, squinting in the bright light reflected from the sand. Lara ran her hand over his damp forehead. "You poor thing, you sounded in such distress, breathing heavily and mumbling something. Were you having the nightmare?"

"I'm going to kill myself."

"Simon. What are you talking about?" said Lara in alarm, "what's wrong?"

He corrected himself quickly and grabbed Lara's hand. "No, not me. I mean me in the nightmare. The person I am in the nightmare. He's going to commit suicide."

"Now remember what Dr Miller said. There's a reason for this nightmare, but that's all it is, a nightmare. None of it is real. You told me you believed there was sense in Dr Miller's theory."

"I don't know, I just don't know for sure. His theory is plausible, but it is just a theory. He hasn't proved anything. Something just doesn't feel right and I'm afraid. I know what's going to happen in the nightmare. He's going to kill himself because he thinks we are two different beings, two separate lives. He thinks he can kill himself and transfer everything he is over to me and my life here."

"But Simon you're talking as if you believe it's all true."

"Because I can't prove it's not true. What if killing himself has some affect on my life. You know how strong the mind is, you've heard of psychosomatic illness and the mind causing disease in the body. If this is all in my mind and a suicide is carried out in my mind within the reality of my nightmare, what's to stop my body reacting accordingly and inducing a heart attack or some other fatal disease that will eventually kill me?"

Lara shifted the parasol to block the sun that was starting to shine on Simon. She knelt in front of him and tried to lighten the expression of concern that threatened to fall across her face. "Let's call Dr Miller today and tell him what's happened. This is significant. He will know what to make of it. I really believe he's on to something and we should let him continue the treatment."

"It's not that I don't have faith in Dr Miller, it's just that he can only treat me from the point of view of a psychotherapist. He said it himself. He's not a metaphysician. He can only treat my mind and if that is where the problem lies, maybe he can help. But I have no way of knowing if the problem is just in my mind. And now things are different. I don't have time to work my way through a theory. My nightmare self is going to commit suicide within the next twenty four hours and I don't know how that is going to affect me."

"Simon, look at it this way, just for the sake of argument, let's say you accept that Dr Miller's theory is correct, that this nightmare is a compensation device from your unconscious to degrade your life in some way and so avert some kind of actual tragedy from talking place. Mentally you have accepted this is just a trick of the unconscious and you have acknowledged what it is trying to tell you. That would mean it has served its purpose and no longer needs to continue the nightmare. So maybe the suicide is the unconscious's way of bringing the nightmare to an end. When the protagonist is dead, the nightmare dies with him. Following Dr Miller's train of thought it makes perfect logical sense, don't you see that?"

"Yes, of course when you put it in that context it does make sense. And I really want to believe that's the way it is Lara, but I'm the one having this thing happening to me. No one knows what it's like living with this hanging over me, unsure of what to believe, unsure of my own judgement even. I wish it wasn't happening and I was like everyone else, but I'm not. I'm trapped between two worlds and no one can help me to break free. Maybe the doctor is right, maybe your suggestion right. But I can't just sit around and wait to see if you're both correct."

"No, we won't just wait. We'll call Dr Miller. In fact let's go and call him now and make an appointment and you can tell him everything you've just told me. We'll see what he makes of it. It's getting too hot on the beach anyway. Let's go inside."

They walked quickly over the hot sand and on to the cooler shaded wood of the terrace. "You're limping Simon. Is your right leg okay?" asked Lara.

"No, it's my foot, it's been this way for a couple of days."

"Let me take a look. Sit on that chair." He sat down and Lara gently held his foot by the ankle. "Where does it hurt?"

"It's the bottom of my foot, near the heel."

She inspected the area and said, "Hmm, I can see something. Just let me get my tweezers." She hurried back with a small pair of eyebrow tweezers. "Now don't move, it might hurt a bit." She manoeuvred the tweezers with the precision of a surgeon and then gently took hold of a dark object. "Here it comes," she said trying to hold her breath at the same time. She held the tweezers and the offending object up into the sunlight. "Wow, no wonder it was hurting you. How long did you say you've had it?"

"I don't know, one or two days I think. I don't remember doing it. What is it?" he said, squinting his eyes to get a closer look.

"It's beautiful," replied Lara, "look at how it sparkles in the sun. It's blue glass, like a tiny fragment of a sapphire. How did you manage to get it in your foot? We don't have any blue glass at home. You must have picked it up on the beach, but I thought you would have known about it at the time, it's quite a sharp piece."

Simon's expression froze. His eyes widened and the blood rushed from his face. Without speaking he reached out to take the tweezers from Lara. He held it up to the light and stared at the shard of blue glass as if it held the secret of life within its sparkle. "Dear God," said Simon slowly and deliberately. "I do remember exactly how I got this in my foot. It happened in the nightmare. I was in the bathroom and I dropped a blue glass tumbler. It shattered on the floor and went everywhere. I couldn't help but stand on it. One piece must have remained lodged in my foot. And now here it is, between these tweezers, transported into my real life." He began to speak excitedly, but the excitement was immersed in a sense of dread. "Lara, Lara, you understand what this means? You see, I told you. It's real. Everything I told you is reality, not in my mind. It's not a nightmare. I was there in that other life as truly as I am here with you now. This glass is the proof. Dear God; Lara, what's happening to me?" He started to shake and his eyes became vacant and staring, mesmerised by the dawning realisation that the foundation of his beliefs of life and death and time and space and creation itself had shattered beyond recognition and something he thought so phenomenally impossible, was not only possible, but was happening in his life now.

Lara protested, "Simon that's not the way it is. You're getting yourself into a panic. You could have picked up the glass anywhere, on the beach, in the ocean, it's just a piece of common blue glass."

"No, you were right the first time. How could I not remember standing on a sharp piece of glass on the beach? It's impossible, it would have made me jump. But I do remember standing on it in the bathroom in the nightmare. It's the living proof Lara. Don't you see what this means. We are one person. Me, here and now and me in that place that disguises itself as my nightmare, we are one and the same, but somehow I travel between these two planes of existence. And now I plan to commit suicide in the nightmare. If I die there, I will die here, in the same way as this blue glass has pierced my foot in both places and causes me physical pain both here and there. My nightmare self has got it all wrong, he things we are separate entities and he can kill himself and not harm me. I've got to stop him Lara. His death is going to kill me too. He's planning it now, in the coming hours. I have to get back to the nightmare now."

"Simon, please stop this. You're becoming unstable and scaring me. Come on, I'm taking you to Dr Miller now, appointment or not, this is an emergency. Come on get dressed."

"Yes, yes, you're right. He's a psychiatrist as well as a psychotherapist. He'll have access to drugs that can sedate me, put me to sleep and back into the nightmare. He could even use hypnosis. That's even better. I might be able to enter the nightmare and still have some consciousness here at the same time. I can stop this suicide."

"No, I don't mean enter the nightmare, I mean Dr Miller can talk you through this." But Simon was not listening. He had already rushed to the bedroom to dress. Within two minutes they were sitting in the car, Lara in the driving seat. "Just stay calm, I'm going to get us there as fast as possible," she said. She turned the key and the engine turned over but died instantly. She repeated it and again the engine whirred and died.

"What's wrong?" screamed Simon.

"I don't know. It was fine yesterday."

She tried again and the engine whirred. Simon held his head in his hands and closed his eyes. On the fourth attempt the engine kicked into life and growled aggressively, but in the same moment his world fell abruptly into complete silence and pitch blackness as he plummeted from the dream.

Chapter Nine

He opened his eyes, but the bedroom was still dark. The growling noise returned, but the sound came from the dogs in the neighbour's garden. He looked across to Rebecca who was still asleep. He smiled to himself. It was Sunday morning, and for him, Sunday night in this life would never come. He crept out of bed and went down to the kitchen. It was just after seven o'clock and Rebecca would not be out of bed for a little while. He had time to think. He sat with a cup of coffee looking out of the window into the grey light of dawn. Rebecca would be out of the house visiting her mother for most of the day but he would only need a few hours to complete his task. The rough sketch of ideas was already being drawn on his mind as dawn crept its way into the kitchen. His single mindedness on the deed he was to perform imbued him with a practical presence of mind, as if he was planning the assembly of a bookshelf rather than the end of his mortal existence. There was something about the imminence of his departure that instilled a lucidity of thought. He felt the surge of creativity that comes in that moment of genius afforded to all who purge their mind of the false imperatives of life and the Illusory charms of the material world. He understood that anyone possessing the foresight to know that in the moment of their final breath, they would see the inconsequentiality of the toil and sweat of their years, and would set their mind free to the coveted and treasured tabula rasa state upon which great ideas may be born. This was the mental state he now enjoyed. And in this state he recognised it was a simple matter of logistics; first he had to sleep, then he had to dream, then he had to die. History and experience had proved that his dreams followed sleep almost instantly. Barely had darkness fallen, when he emerged into the golden light of the dream. This part would be easy. In fact Rebecca would help him, although quite inadvertently and without her knowledge or consent. She had a rich supply of *Zolpidem* pills, guaranteed to put a horse to sleep she would say. He would take four or five of those to render him unconscious and allow the dream process to begin. As soon as he felt himself starting to fall asleep he would engage the process of death in the form of carbon monoxide poisoning. A simple turn of the car ignition key in his drug induced drowsy state and he would leave the rest to the indomitable laws of nature that govern the rules of life and death within the human body. The car will be in the garage with everything suitably airtight and nothing would stop him. Except... He thought back to his last dream. He knew his dream self was going to attempt to stop him. But how could he? He had no influence away from his own realm of existence. Whatever he tried would fail. He could not transgress the laws that were controlling their lives. But all the same he would not allow him the luxury of time. In a few hours it would all be over, and then there would be nothing that anyone could do.

Rebecca was particularly talkative during the morning as she readied herself to leave for the day. She was almost pleasant in a perfunctory sort of way as if she might have sensed she would never see him again and should make their final mutual moments as civil as possible. There were brief moments when he wanted to tell her everything; to just let it out. He could hear the words in his mind, *Rebecca. While you're out I am going to take five of your Zolpidem tablets, then asphyxiate myself in the Renault. Do you want me to leave you any dinner?* He smiled to himself, not out of humour but out of the little victory that he will have scored when all this is over. He just wished he could be here to witness the aftermath of his death; to see Rebecca, perhaps revealing her true sentiments, whatever they may be; to see his children regretting their instinctive need for rebellion and perturbing his onset of middle age. Most of all to see Damien and maybe witness him admit he was wrong to refuse helping a friend to do what he was going to do anyway; wrong to cast a moral judgement against him and wrong not to simply accept him for whom he was in life. But soon these things will be sentiments of the past, consigned to history and the eulogies penned by those left behind and none of it will have any bearing on the life that awaits him.

At twelve o'clock sharp, the sound of a car horn signalled the arrival Rebecca's brother who would take her as usual to their mother's house for the day. Simon watched as she put on her coat, picked up her house keys and muttered a cursory goodbye without looking back. It seemed fitting that his last impression of her would be one of indifference. He felt no sentiment in that moment. He was not sure whether it was because none had existed for so long in the frigid dark waters in which their marriage floundered or because any sentiment he possessed was already being channelled into the new life that awaited him.

He waited for the car to drive away and at last he sat alone in the house. He briefly wondered about leaving a suicide note; although it was not really a suicide, it would be more of a farewell letter. Suicide had a greater sense of ending about it, whereas he was about to embark on what was really a new beginning. But whatever the missive should be called, he decided against it. Everything that needed to be said had already been said to Damien. Rebecca would probably burn the letter and he doubted if the children would have the faculty of mind to be able to read it in the spirit in which it was written.

He went outside and drove the Renault into the garage. The petrol tank was half full; approximately twenty five litres. He remembered from human biology lessons at school that the average adult lung capacity was about six litres, so he reckoned he could fill his lungs to capacity and still have nineteen litres of petrol as reserve. He smiled to himself at the absurdity of the calculation. He had no idea how much carbon monoxide it would take to complete the job. If only the maths problems he was set at school had been more practical. Instead of the usual unimaginative questions such as, *how many men does it take to dig a hole two metres deep*, they should have posed more real-world and creative challenges such as, *how many litres of regular unleaded does it take to render a depressed adult male stone cold dead?* That might have stirred some interest among the vacuous number phobics as they chewed their pencils. He let out a laugh and did not try to stifle it. Why should he? There was nothing solemn about this moment; which made him wonder if all suicide candidates commonly experienced humorous observations and laughter as they constructed the apparatus of their self inflicted execution. Probably not he surmised; theirs was a grim task born of pain and suffering. Their motivation was the oblivion of their torment, with the erasure of their past and present prevailing over any thought or desire of a future destination. For him it was different. He was erasing his past and present too, but he was stepping across the boundary of time and space into his beautiful future. He had a destination. This was not a suicide, despite what the coroner's report would say. But was it possible that his laughter came from a different place, not a place of humour but from a place of nervousness and anxiety? Taking one's life successfully was a once in a lifetime event; he had no personal experience to draw upon for how it would feel. It irritated him that the whole affair had to be so theatrical. Why could the objective not be achieved by way of a simple statement of intention like deciding to quit smoking or grow old gracefully or just go to sleep? But that really is all it was, it was just falling asleep. He had opted not to go for the drama of a gunshot to the head or to languish in a warm bath tinted scarlet red as blood seeped from his artery. He was not making a statement and did not need to glorify the moment with an act of extravagant violence. He was going the way of sleep; some painless pills, some painless vapours and it would all be over. And with that assurance, the nervous laughter drained away.

But thinking about the school maths problems brought his thoughts round to his children. In a short while they would be fatherless but that knowledge did not unsettle him. They were sharp, independently minded street-wise survivors. They had already asserted their independence and made no secret of the fact that they saw parents as a burden and something to tolerate, not revere or share their lives with. Gavin was bright and tough and did not need authority to hold his hand. He would see his father's death as a badge of honour; once he had embellished the details a little. He would share the *truth* of his suicide with his drug touting friends, omitting the fact he died from the exhaust fumes of his blue Renault and replacing it with an overdose of whatever the most notorious street drug of the moment was. He would become a Jimi Hendrix or Marilyn Monroe; a legend, masquerading in the conservative guise of an accountant for reasons best known to him and a secret society whose name cannot be spoken. As for Mandy, she will relish in that she has one less obstacle to negotiate in her campaign to escape from Wessingdon Hill and all it entails, and who could blame her. She was thirteen years old with the mind of twenty year old; an opinionated, acerbic force of one and heaven help anyone who stood in her way: it definitely would not be him. Neither of them needed an under achieving accountant father as a guide or role model. They were rebels: let them rebel and if they rebelled long enough and were rebellious enough maybe they would fare better than their father did. He looked at his watch, snapping himself out of his thoughts. He was wasting time in idle reflections.

In one corner of the garage he sifted through four large heavy duty cardboard boxes. Each was filled to the brim with the miscellaneous paraphernalia that amasses over the years, but in the bottom box was the thing that he wanted; a three metre section of washing machine hose. He never could bring himself to throw it away for some reason, but today its true purpose had been revealed. In one of the other boxes was a half used roll of grey duct tape. He closed the double garage doors to preserve his privacy from the road outside and then placed one end of the hose over the end of the exhaust pipe. The hose was a wider bore than the exhaust pipe but he bound it several times with the duct tape until he had achieved a secure tight seal. He then fed the other end of the hose through the partially open driver's door window and then closed it sufficiently until it held the hose securely. Using some more duct tape he sealed the remaining gaps in the partially open window until he was happy that it was as airtight as possible. He stood back and admired the innovation of his self styled execution chamber. It was more Heath Robinson than NASA, but it was practical and expedient.

He locked the garage doors and went back inside the house. From the bathroom cabinet he counted out five *Zolpidem* tablets, then went into the bedroom and grabbed some woollen jumpers. Finally he took a small bottle of water from the fridge and the black umbrella from the hat stand in the hallway, then took one last look around the house and left it for the last time. Unlocking the garage doors he was about to swing them open when a voice carried from his left side. "Afternoon Simon. Feeling the cold today?"

He looked around, startled by the voice. It was his next door neighbour. For a moment he was puzzled by the comment, but tried to act naturally. Then he realised the attempted humour as he looked at the bundle of woollen jumpers in his arms."Oh, er, no, no, just some old things I'm putting into storage." He paused until the neighbour had walked away, then opened the garage doors and went inside quickly, closing and locking the doors with the two bolts from the inside. He wedged the woollen jumpers within the gaps of the doors, eliminating as much air flow as was possible with his makeshift draught proofing. He snapped the handle off the umbrella, discarding it on the ground, then took what was left of the umbrella and entered the Renault from the passenger side. Depressing the accelerator pedal all the way to the floor he positioned the tip of the broken umbrella on the pedal and wedged the other end into the lower part of the driver's seat. This forced the accelerator pedal down permanently which would allow for the maximum amount of fumes to enter the car as quickly as possible.

And now the scene was set. He slid into the driver's seat being careful not to touch the umbrella, then inserted the key into the ignition. In the palm of his hand were the five oval, pale blue tablets. He stared at them and pondered on the magnitude of these innocuous looking little slabs of chalk. Everything depended on these tablets putting him into a dream filled sleep and keeping him there until the exhaust fumes made his sleep permanent. But then the first doubts arose. Should he test the tablets first, maybe trying different quantities and assessing how long they took to induce sleep? This might be safer, but time was not on his side. He would not have the house to himself again until the following Sunday and so much could happen before then. He was already aware that he was now competing; competing with himself, with his dream self who at this moment was trying to banish him from his existence with the help of a psychotherapist. He feared what they could achieve together. He was starting to panic and quickly tossed all five tablets into this mouth, swallowing them down with the bottle of water. He grimaced at their bitter, chalky taste and then sat back in the seat breathing heavily. He looked at his watch. It was ten to one. Rebecca said the tablets often worked within fifteen minutes. He closed his eyes and tried to forget the time and relax himself into the end of his current life.

He thought of Lara. Soon he would be with her, but this time it would be forever. No more being wrenched from the beauty of his days and nights with her. Soon they would be married. They would toast their future from the top of the lighthouse on the beach. They would spend the rest of their lives basking in the golden light of the Californian sun and they would sail through turquoise oceans in their yacht, the *Spirit of Lara* and when the time came they would retire to a small island in the Caribbean and grow old elegantly watching their grandchildren play in the white sand.

His old life had already passed into the chronicles of his spent days; days of which he had no desire to reminisce; days which held no lasting treasure for his mind. What had passed could now be consigned to the shadowy archives of the forgotten, and there, may they rest or rot, for they were of little consequence from this moment on.

And as his mind returned to the Pacific breeze caressing the sunlit terrace of the beach house he felt the first jolt of impending sleep. He glanced at his watch. Twenty minutes had passed and he felt waves of sleep surging through his body. He tried to hold on a few minutes more, until he was certain that sleep was taking him, but to wait too long might also be to leave it too late. Again his body jolted as sleep nudged him once more and he decided this was the moment. Keeping his eyes closed, he felt for the ignition key and twisted it clockwise. The depressed accelerator pedal surged the engine into life and the process had begun. Simon's hand dropped from the key and his head flopped to the side, resting on the window close to the hose. He could hear the growl of the engine and smell the fumes, but it was vague and confused as the drugs held him in a fatal soporific state. As seconds passed, the sounds began to fade away and the curtain began to fall and Simon fell into a drug induced toxic sleep.

Chapter Ten

"No, no, David don't bring me out of it yet. He's doing it now, he's killing himself," mumbled Simon.

David Miller replied calmly, "I'm not bringing you out of the hypnotic state Simon, you're doing it yourself. It's your own will bringing you out."

Simon's eyes opened. He sat in the same chair he occupied the first time he visited Dr Miller. "No, it's not me doing it." Simon insisted. "I was forced out of the nightmare. He's in the car now with the exhaust fumes trailing in through the window; he's poisoning himself. You've got to put me under again; you have to get me back there before he dies."

"Simon I can try to put you into a hypnotic state again, but you if you fail to respond, I cannot force you."

"Then use a drug. You can anaesthetise me; hurry I'm running out of time."

"No Simon, I don't have those facilities here and anyway, ethically and medically I cannot just render you unconscious so you can enter a dream state. You must understand I am only conducting this hypnotherapy session in an attempt to reach your unconscious and find out why this is happening."

Simon dismissed his explanation irritably, what did he care for his ethics if it cost him his life. "Yes, anything, just try to put me back under."

David Miller for the second time took Simon into the hypnotic state. "Where are you Simon? What can you see?"

Simon was agitated. He rolled his head from side to side in the chair and spoke in a delirious state. "It's getting dark, I'm travelling in the dark. I can smell...." and as his words faded away, he slipped deeper into the darkness of his nightmare.

Chapter Eleven

Simon's eyes opened wide. The car was full of smoke. He gasped and inhaled a lungful of fumes. He screamed out, "No, leave me alone. Let me die. You can't keep me away from Lara. You can't keep me from my life." He felt his hand instinctively reaching for the ignition key. He was seized by a desire that impelled him to reach out and turn off the engine. Maybe it was the choking fumes and instinct for bodily survival, but he fought the urge and again he spluttered the words through the toxic haze "leave me to die, so I can live." His words, desperate and anguished were loud enough to carry above the roar of the engine and beyond the garage doors.

"Simon, is that you? Simon, answer me," Damien yelled. He banged on the doors with his fists and shouted again, "Simon open these doors." He saw wisps of dirty grey smoke seeping out through the cracks in the doors and his heart lurched as he realised the truth of what was happening and the dread of what he would find beyond the wooden doors; for they were all that stood between the continuing life of his best friend and the burden of guilt and remorse that he would carry for eternity if he could not break through. He looked around frantically for something to prise open the door, but was almost knocked off his feet as Simon's neighbour suddenly appeared wielding a pick axe above his head.

"Stand back," the man yelled and proceeded to hack away at the doors in what looked like a crazed frenzy. Damien stood back, watching helplessly, feeling useless and frantic.

"Strike the centre of the doors, where the locks are," shouted Damien. "If you weaken them we can kick the door in." But the neighbour was oblivious to instruction and continued to swipe erratically at the doors.

Damien became desperate and tried to grab the axe, but could not get close enough without the risk of being struck. Finally he yelled, "get out of the way, stand back, I'm going to try something."

From inside the car Simon heard the muffled sound of Damien's voice and the hammering on the doors. In his confused state, he spoke wearily, his voice barely audible. "Damien no, please don't come in. Please, not now. I'm so close. Let me go." The last words of his sentence were drowned out by the sound of the garage doors splintering open as Damien drove his car into them. Simon heard the crash and felt the impact of Damien's car hit the back of the Renault. But the *Zolpidem* and the exhaust fumes were invading and compromising his system and as Damien fought his way through the broken doors and grabbed the hose, wrenching it out of the window, Simon's eyes rolled back and he fell into darkness.

Chapter Twelve

"Simon, I'm now going to bring you out of your sleep very gently," said David Miller. Simon gasped for air, a feint hiss coming from deep in his throat. His hands clutched at his chest and throat as if desperate for air. Lara sat in the seat next to him. "Dr Miller, what's happening, he looks like he's suffocating. Bring him out of it quickly."

For the first time, David Miller betrayed a hint of concern; his voice still composed, but his tone higher and more urgent. "Simon, you are quite safe. You are with Dr Miller, safe and comfortable in the office. I am now bringing you out of sleep and when I do you will be completely well and refreshed and rested. I am counting down from ten, nine, eight, seven, six and now you are coming up, rising back to your normal waking self, waking up from sleep." Simon continued to breathe erratically in short laboured spurts.

"Doctor bring him out of it, bring him back, he's suffocating," panicked Lara.

David Miller looked at her nervously, his eyes suffused with uncertainty. The usual confidence that graced his professional persona now seemed to elude him as his patient diverged from the expected pattern of behaviour. With the tremulous taint of consternation in his voice he continued to count down, "Five, four, three, two, one and you are now awake and relaxed and safe."

Simon stopped breathing.

The room had become dark, but the blinds were wide open and revealed through the window a billowing swarm of dense black cloud that swept across the sky obscuring the Californian sun and its life-giving warm light. It brought with it winds from the east that blew cold and sharp and within the wind it carried moisture that formed rain that fell in watery slivers, icy and stinging and indiscriminate. And the air pulsed with the charge of a latent storm, threatening and ominous and in its atmosphere was the sense of a different place, not of the west coast with its light and its warmth but of a place in the east and to the north where the cloud hangs heavy and dark, fuelled by the smoke of industry that lay below it.

In the growing darkness Dr Miller leaned over Simon, whose eyes were closed. His body was rigid, lifeless; he exuded the aura of a corpse, devoid of the subtle nuances that signalled the warm, vibrant surges of life. His wan complexion, drawn and bloodless painted him in a ghostly pallor. In the dense silence of the room no sound emanated from Simon's body; neither the whisper of breath, nor the muffled throb of a beating heart. The air that shrouded him lay cold and stagnant and heavy. Lara jumped up out of her chair and fell to the side of Simon. David Miller threw up his hand to stop her touching him. He held her arm, restraining her without making eye contact and stared motionless at the face of his patient who cast a grim pose of death.

Lara fought tears that threatened to flood from terrified eyes. This was her doing. She dragged him to this doctor who told him his tragedy was an illusion that dwelt in his mind. She told the man she loved that portents of his death were the morbid figments of dark but benign shadows of dreams, nothing but the sinister impressions of nightmares that fade harmlessly with the coming of the dawn light. She and this doctor doubted his truth; they disparaged his claims with their superior assertions and betrayed his anguished plea for help. She turned to Dr Miller, snatching her arm free from his grip and they both looked at each other in a stare of silent disbelief. But the stare was broken by a subtle movement glimpsed in the corner of their eyes.

Simon's eyes flicked opened. He breathed in a long slow sonorous breath as if drawing the first breath of mortal life. He looked cautiously around the room.

"You're safe Simon" said David Miller.

"He did it," said Simon. "He did it. I think he's dead. I was too late, I couldn't stop him."

The psychotherapist had regained his full composure. His voice was firm, measured and any trace of vulnerability banished to the annals of experience. "But you are still here Simon," he said. "You are still alive. And that tells me that there *was* a death, but it was not you. Your death was something that you feared, but it was the death of your fear that took place; the fear your unconscious brought up from the depths within you. It's dead Simon, the nightmare is dead and you can start to move forward and recover from this point on."

"Can I really? How do I know it's over? How do I know the nightmare has come to an end? I can't be sure that he's dead. His friend, Damien was there in the last seconds. He could have revived him. And even if he is dead, how do I know his death has not triggered the process of my own death, some ticking time bomb that has started its countdown within me."

David Miller leaned forward and spoke with a deep sense of compassion. "The fact is Simon, nothing is certain. Time will tell if the nightmare is over. But you are still thinking in terms of competition and conflict with another individual rather than the conflict with an aspect of yourself. We still have a lot of work to do and over the sessions that lie ahead of us we will work through these issues."

On the drive home, Simon was silent. The latent storm never materialised and a cordial blue sky hung over them. Lara glanced at him periodically, attempting to speak, then realised there was nothing she could say that had not already been said. In bed that night he stared through the open windows at the half moon suspended in a twilight sky. A soft breeze ruffled the curtains, but nothing else disturbed the silence of the room. Lara lay by his side, sensing his apprehension, watching the tension mount on his face as he waited and feared the inevitability of sleep. As the night drifted on, the wind strengthened and stirred the air in the room but Simon lay still, cradled in Lara's watchful embrace. When the first dappled light of dawn played over the ceiling, Simon wearily opened his eyes and looked around the room. It was the same familiar room with large French windows looking on to the ocean outside. Lara lay by his side, her chestnut mane twirled and tousled over his chest and her devotion to him tangible in the currents of salubrious air that surrounded them. There had been no nightmare, not even a dream, just the flat, silent oblivion of unconscious sleep.

And on the next night, sleep came again in untroubled drifts of restful peace. And so it was, night after night, the hours of darkness untrammelled by the world of nightmares: and dreams; only of the innocuous substance of life's daily trivialities.

His mind sometimes mused on those weeks over which the nightmares took place. He grew to accept that he was not going to die because of a suicide in a nightmare. At times he even wondered if that person in the nightmare had achieved his objective and killed himself and his bleak life and was now living the dream life he always wanted within this, his own body and mind here on the Californian coastline. But that was a pointless and even damaging mental exercise. It was impossible to prove and David Miller had successfully persuaded him to lay the notion to rest. The sessions with Dr Miller continued for just over a year and came to a natural conclusion when both men felt that peace had been restored to the psyche and harmony had a foundation of fertile ground in which to flourish.

When Simon and Lara were married they blessed the day of their wedding and the remaining days of their lives from the top of the lighthouse overlooking the pacific. They sailed the world on their honeymoon voyage in the *Spirit of Lara* and the perfect days that embodied their life together seemed carved into the stone tablets of their destiny.

Chapter Thirteen

It was almost two years after the nightmares ended, on a cool misty morning that Simon sat on the terrace wearing a fleeced, hooded top to keep out the early chill. He had been there since dawn, mesmerised by the phenomenon that was the birth of the sea mist. It formed within the fledgling rays of early sunlight; so innocuous at first; beautiful, yet insignificant strands of white vapour that flowed out of the dawn light, their nebulous tendrils twisting around each other to form larger swirls of silvery haze. The rising sun, growing in intensity stared into the mist, burning the veil that draped itself across the sky like a gossamer breath, but as the minutes passed the white vapour grew and melded into a dense white cloud that rose like a vengeful phantom out of the ocean, morphing its vague, undulating body into grasping claws that choked the sun and stifled the light until its ghostly form cloaked the day in a luminous aura of cold, stark emptiness. Perhaps there was an ill omen in the mist that morning, for in the announcement of its coming it brought with it a tide of dark change.

As he sipped his coffee he shuddered instinctively, almost dropping the cup. The cause was a report in the first column on page six of the Los Angeles Times. It stated two media celebrities from a network television channel had been killed in a boating accident off the Gulf of Mexico. What caused him to shudder were not the identities of the celebrities, whom he did not know, but the vessel. It was a yacht called *Meridian* and was one of Simon's newly launched fleet which he had christened the *Swordfish* series, boasting a new and innovative design and using new, state of the art materials. Over the coming days a successful salvage operation was launched for the recovery of the yacht, which instigated a full investigation into the cause of the tragedy. It was implied that the yacht's revolutionary new hull design in combination with the new composite material was responsible for catastrophically compromising the hull, causing enough instability in the hands of a novice crew in challenging weather to bring about the yacht's demise. But before the findings could be published, a second of Simon's *Swordfish* series yachts came to grief off the coast of Australia in heavy weather. Three people aboard the *Maisy Blue* died; two from drowning and one from head injuries sustained during the incident. Blame was attributed once again to the combination of radical new hull design and its composite material. Following the second tragedy, all of the new *Swordfish* series of yachts had their certificates of seaworthiness revoked pending review. It was the beginning of a traumatic time of inquests, investigations, hearings and accusations. Multiple court actions were brought against Simon and his company, including charges of negligence, gross professional incompetence and unlawful killing. Most charges were eventually dropped on the grounds of inconclusive evidence and two professional contradictory theories that polarised the matter in the minds of the governing bodies and courts. But the residue of doubt and ambiguity left behind was enough to initiate the rapid decline and subsequent collapse of his company. Sales for all yachts bearing his company name, regardless of type came to an abrupt end.

It signalled the start of a long night of treachery within the maritime world. Like wolves, the competition formed packs, and smelling the blood of the weakened and injured party they circled and probed and inflicted the wounds that led to the final kill. Even those who would be called friends and colleagues sensed the fear in the air and recoiled lest they should be tainted by the poisonous slur of professional failure. At worst he was seen as a liability and at best a bad omen in an industry entrenched in superstition.

The legal costs served jointly as punishment and insult. Though jurisprudence had not found him guilty of any crime, he suffered the penalty of crippling costs which were incurred in order to defend his name and reputation. With no income, business debts in the form of ruthless debtors, and severed lifelines from the banks who lauded him so effusively in good times, he was forced to declare bankruptcy. Although the beach house was protected from seizure in the bankruptcy proceedings, it eventually had to be sold along with his other personal assets. From the abundant pool of friends, colleagues, business associates and general sycophants who promulgated their presence during the times of plenty, all that remained were the most shameless vultures who picked at the bones of what remained.

The period of time from that first ominous newspaper report on that inauspicious grey morning to the culmination of financial ruin was just under two and a half years and in that time Simon had become reclusive and unresponsive to all attempts to pacify or motivate him. Lara battled with his darkening decline, her own fortitude besieged by the assault of so many adversaries in the external world and sabotaged by the black moods that defined her internal world, until the inevitable defeat devoured her too. The strain on their marriage eroded its now fragile foundation and as the cracks appeared, then widened, they realised the seeds of destruction had been sown and the survival of their relationship hung precariously, like autumn leaves awaiting the first gusts of October. But so long ago in those early days of newness and hope, the words and sentiments they proclaimed of undying love formed the lifeblood of their union; words and sentiments that fell so easily from their lips, yet were so hard to enact once hardship entered their lives. And as the bitterness and harsh realities of their changing world lacerated their bond, the lifeblood seeped away through the open wounds of neglect and abandonment until their love slowly bled to death and all that remained was the forgotten memory of a once eternal promise. Lara moved out of their rented accommodation taking what few possessions she had left to her name. These did not include the diamond engagement ring she so treasured, which had been sold many months earlier to cover legal debts.

As Simon stood in the shadows, concealed by the broken blinds of a bedroom window and watched Lara walk away from his world, he knew she would return. He knew with a knowing as certain as death itself that she would come back to him; maybe later that same evening or if not that evening, the next day or perhaps the following week; certainly no later than the following month. But as one month drifted into three months, the knowing faded and changed. It transformed and reduced to belief; belief that Lara would not desert him. As six months passed, the belief faded too and transformed into hope; that desperate virtue afforded to those without power or influence, and in the tenth month of Lara's absence hope finally died and gave way to truth; the simple grave truth that Lara was gone.

And now Simon sat alone in his rented one room apartment in the rundown part of the cheaper end of town. He drank more than he should, but it blunted the pain and obscured the mind from the memories of days when life was adorned in satins and silks and the gods rained prosperity over their charmed lives. Some nights he drank so much that he forgot almost everything; everything except Lara. She was always there, mingling the sweet memory of her face with the bitter torture of her absence. He could have coped with losing everything but her; but now her memory; the memory of her loss merely proclaimed his abysmal failure and the depth to which he had sunk.

But it was not long before something wrestled him out of his daily reverie. Usually it was the demand for the weeks rent which became increasingly difficult to find. It was often a trade off between being able to afford enough alcohol to stifle his senses from reality or paying the rent to avoid being thrown out onto the street. But this decision was taken out of his hands one Friday night when a homemade petrol bomb came hurtling through his window. He managed to put out the ensuing fire but the damage was excessive; given the already decrepit state of the apartment. It seemed that anonymity had not followed him on his downward spiral in life. The morning following the petrol bomb attack saw the delivery of a crude hand scrawled note levelling charges of murder against him and claiming a travesty of justice in the court's failure to arrive at a guilty verdict in the yachting tragedies. The apartment landlord promptly evicted him on the grounds that he was a liability he could not afford.

His latest abode was of even less glamorous a nature than the previous one and in order to afford the rent he was now in that most undesirable part of town whose denizens were the fallen, the wayward and victims of sheer misfortune. Although as with most of life's adversities there were unexpected compensations. As a result of his daunting location, it was not long before he was approached one night in the shadowy doorway of a boarded up liquor store and offered a fully serviced hand gun with six rounds at a very competitive price. Its impromptu salesman, an enthusiastic and impressive drifter of life's more desperate avenues assured him with blood curdling conviction that it was lightweight, easy to conceal, and for its size, packed considerable stopping power. It was too good an offer to turn down and Simon purchased it without hesitation using the week's rent money.

That same night he lay on his bed. It was hard to sleep as the neon lights from the strip club across the street flashed continuously through his window. There were no curtains, but he tore the bed sheet in two and hung one piece over part of the window. It only served to diffuse the light though and filled the whole room with alternating orange and blue washes of colour. Sleep would not come, but he never forced it these days. After all, there was nothing particular to get up for in the morning.

He held the loaded gun across his chest. Tonight he was ready for them. If they had managed to trace him to this address and hurled another petrol bomb through the window, he would rush out there and would use all six rounds if necessary. If they really thought he was a murderer, he would give them just cause for their accusation. He smiled to himself. It was a victory of sorts. It was primitive, but this time he would have the means to fight back and come out on top. But at the same time he knew this was not his natural behaviour and the thought troubled him. It led him to reflect on the would-be assassin's motives. Maybe they were right. Perhaps there was some justice in their action. Five people were dead. They claim it was because of his negligence.

Maybe it was. Maybe he became too arrogant and took risks that other people would have to account for. The courts ruled in his favour, but only because of insufficient evidence. He always felt the prosecution lawyers were weak. A hotshot lawyer would have been different. He would have moulded the evidence to fit the charge. He would have coaxed and manipulated the jury and had them performing for him. Then there would have been a guilty verdict and the deaths of five people would have been mitigated by the conviction of their slayer, for even though he had no intent, death was death regardless of the thought process behind its orchestration. Why should he still live and breathe while those innocent parties who put their faith in the integrity of a marine architect lost their lives. Anyway, what good did an acquittal do him? He still lost everything he ever owned, everything he ever valued. And what was he left with? The one thing he did not value at all: his own futile life. What point was there in being left alive to breathe if the only air to breathe was tainted by the putrid stench of decay? The smell of decline and corruption was everywhere; in the festering streets outside, in his room, in his bed, in the tattered clothes that hung over his tired body. The courts should have served justice; they should have found him guilty of incompetence, negligence, dereliction of duty, betrayal of the woman he loved, disregard for the sanctity of life and unlawful killing. And what penalty would best serve such a multitude of misdeeds? None that could appease his craving for his own dismissal from everything he had ever known.

But then he realised he alone could enforce what the court could not. He had the method at his disposal and required no authority beyond that which he held across his chest; the dirty black Glock 19 pistol. It smelled of lubricating oil mixed with the acrid scent of execution. In a single moment he could wipe the slate clean, deliver justice to five innocent lives and erase the canvas of his own life. He raised the Glock and held the barrel to his temple. It felt cold against his skin; cold and physically shocking like a pre-emptive taste of what it could do if the desire was supported by a strong enough will.

From somewhere in his mind the thought of David Miller suddenly materialised. It seemed like a lifetime ago when his biggest problem was a simple nightmare. What would Dr Miller think of the situation now? How would he resolve this one? It would have been so simple if the nightmares had continued but at the same time there had been no change to the perfect days of his life. After all, what was a nightmare but a dark figment of the sleeping mind. It could do him no harm. But it came to an end in Dr Miller's office one grey afternoon. And that posed a question that raged in his mind; was that why his whole world came crashing down? Because the nightmare ended, leaving his privileged existence exposed to the world and its malignant forces. But in fact the nightmare had not come to an end at all. It just went through a transformation. His beautiful life had faded away, his existence vaporised. He had experienced the evanescence of being, and what remained in this new dark and disturbed reality were the vile things of nightmares.

He pressed the pistol against his head and caressed the trigger gently, the way he might have stroked a faithful hound, knowing he would not let him down when the time came. The reflections of the orange and blue lights that painted the ceiling were distracting, but also mildly comforting. They carried him back to memories of the bedroom at the beach house when the orange glow of the early sunrise danced on the ceiling and the cold blue of the moonlight cooled the night. For a moment he smelled the scent of Lara's hair and tasted the sweetness of her skin and the cool wet touch of her lips; so different to the touch of the cool violent barrel of the Glock. He smiled again. He was so tired, so infinitely tired. He tightened his grip on the pistol and closed his eyes. He felt waves of sleep carrying him away, deep into the realms of unconsciousness and as sleep completely consumed him he crossed the threshold into his dream world.

Chapter Fourteen

His eyes opened slowly. He was sitting in his favourite leather armchair next to the marble fireplace. The deep ticking of the grandfather clock lent a warm oaky ambience to the room but it was suddenly muted by the shrill ring of the phone. He was about to leap up and answer it when the door opened and Victoria rushed in, "I'll get it darling, I didn't want it to disturb you." She picked up the phone, "Hello........No I'm sorry, the doctor's not available this afternoon." She looked at Simon in his chair and winked knowingly at him. "Oh, it's you Mrs Thorpe...... Yes I did mention to my husband that you'd like him to say a few words at your association luncheon. But it's probably best if you call him at the surgery tomorrow, after surgery hours; he'll have his appointment diary then........No, don't worry, it's no trouble." She put the phone down and sighed. "Honestly, you'd think you were the only doctor in the county. That Mrs Thorpe wants you to do a talk about prescription drugs and teenage depression." She skipped over to Simon and sat on his lap. "This village relies on you too much. They all say you're the best doctor they've had in sixty years. They won't even take an aspirin without checking with you first. I must be the luckiest girl in the world to be married to the best doctor in Sussex, who's also handsome, charming, kind, generous and...."

".... And hungry," said Simon. "Is lunch ready?"

"Fifteen minutes. I just have to open the wine." She leapt up and took a bottle of red wine from the sideboard. As she opened it, Simon watched her. The sun was streaming in through the drawing room windows and appeared to radiate a glow around her shock of short blonde hair. Her hairstyle gave her a cheeky, impish look, but this was countered by the innate seduction in her emerald eyes; sharp and green like the stone from which they took their hue and tapered sensuously to a sharp point that gave her gaze an enigmatic feline quality. Her gait too was cat-like and she appeared to stroke the ground on which she walked, each movement of her lithe form made deliberately and with precision.

As she uncorked the wine, the door flew open again and Felicity bounded into the room, every bit as radiant and golden as her mother. She jumped onto Simon's lap. "Daddy, daddy, I thought of a name for my new pony. I'm going to call him Henry. Is that a good name?"

"I think it's a wonderful name for a pony. Yes, you should definitely call him Henry," smiled Simon as he kissed her nose.

"Felicity, go and wash your hands and tell your brother too, lunch is nearly ready," said Victoria. Felicity ran out of the room and Victoria jumped back into Simon's lap, twirling his hair around her finger as she spoke, "And now Dr Simon, before we eat, have you arranged for holiday cover for the surgery for next month. The children are so excited about skiing for the first time."

"No, I haven't had a chance but I'll get them to sort it out tomorrow, I promise."

"I do worry about you darling. You seem so tired these days. You must give yourself the same care that you give your patients. Life is so perfect for all of us. We have a beautiful family, this wonderful home in the prettiest county in England and you are so highly respected within your profession, but what would we do if something happened to you? All of it would be meaningless without you. You're my soul mate and I could never live without you."

"And you know I could never live without you, you are my whole world. Life is perfect darling. We're so lucky; it's just that I'm not sleeping so well."

"Why? Is something bothering you?"

"Oh, it's nothing. Just a silly dream; well more of a nightmare I suppose."

"A nightmare? You never told me."

"It's nothing. I didn't want to worry you. I'm just having this sort of ongoing nightmare."

"What kind of nightmare?"

"It's really strange. I have a completely different life with different people. I live in America. I was a marine architect, designing these amazing super yachts, then something went wrong. Two of the yachts I designed sunk, killing some people. I lost my company and was declared bankrupt, losing everything I had. Then my wife left me and I became an alcoholic. I've had death threats, I live in some kind of ghetto and I think I'm toying with the idea of shooting myself with a gun I bought from a desperate looking character in the street."

"Simon, that's the most horrible thing I've ever heard. Why would you have nightmares like that? I told you, you're working far too hard. After the skiing holiday I want you to cut back on your surgery hours. We don't need the money and you need more time with your family. Who's that nice doctor you introduced me to at the polo ball last summer, you know, the psychotherapist one. Why don't you have a talk with him about the nightmares, it probably just needs talking through with someone who knows about these things."

"No, I don't need to talk to anyone. I just need a rest; the skiing holiday will do me good."

"Okay, whatever you think is best; you're the doctor, but I just want you to take care of yourself. I know the holiday is just what you need, we're going to have a wonderful time. But please promise me you'll try not to worry, remember it's not real, it's just a nightmare".

"Yes I know sweetheart, I promise. I know it's not real, it's just a nightmare".